Reading and Interpreting the Works of

THE BRONTË SISTERS

Enslow Publishing

101 W. 23rd Street
Suite 240
New York, NY 10011
USA

enslow.com

Lit Crit Guides

Reading and Interpreting the Works of

THE BRONTË SISTERS

Naomi Pasachoff

Published in 2018 by Enslow Publishing, LLC
101 W. 23rd Street, Suite 240, New York, NY 10011

Library of Congress Cataloging-in-Publication Data
Names: Pasachoff, Naomi E., author.
Title: Reading and interpreting the works of the Brontë sisters / Naomi Pasachoff.
Description: First edition. | New York, NY : Enslow Publishing, 2018. | Series: Lit crit guides. | Includes bibliographical references and index. | Audience: Grades 7-12.
Identifiers: LCCN 2016057576 | ISBN 9780766089495 (library bound : alk. paper)
Subjects: LCSH: Brontë, Charlotte, 1816-1855--Criticism and interpretation—Juvenile literature. | Brontë, Emily, 1818-1848--Criticism and interpretation—Juvenile literature. | Brontë, Anne, 1820-1849--Criticism and interpretation—Juvenile literature.
Classification: LCC PR4168 .P288 2018 | DDC 823/.8--dc23
LC record available at https://lccn.loc.gov/2016057576

Printed in China

10 9 8 7 6 5 4 3 2 1

To Our Readers: We have done our best to make sure all website addresses in this book were active and appropriate when we went to press. However, the author and the publisher have no control over and assume no liability for the material available on those websites or on any websites they may link to. Any comments or suggestions can be sent by e-mail to customerservice@enslow.com.

Portions of this book originally appeared in *A Student's Guide to the Brontë Sisters*.

Photo Credits: Cover, pp. 3, 6 Fine Art/Corbis Historical/Getty Images; pp. 11, 43, 120, 133 Christopher Furlong/Getty Images; pp. 15, 146 Loop Images/Universal Images Group/Getty Images; p. 20 Rischgitz/Hulton Archive/Getty Images; p. 25 Monty Fresco/Hulton Archive/Getty Images; p. 30 British Library/Wikimedia; p. 33 Photo by Jay Pasachoff, Charlotte Brontë, "Lord's Prayer 1835," HM 33702, The Huntington Library, San Marino, California; pp. 40, 47, 55, 64, 102, 135 Culture Club/Hulton Archive/Getty Images; p. 59 Print Collector/Hulton Archive/Getty Images; p. 71 Hulton Archive/Getty Images; p. 76 Pictorial Press Ltd/Alamy Stock Photo; pp. 80, 97 Time Life Pictures/The LIFE Picture Collection/Getty Images; p. 84 VisitBritain/Britain on View/Getty Images; p. 91 Michael Ochs Archives/Getty Images; p. 93 Andy Lidstone/Shutterstock.com; p. 111 The Keasbury-Gordon Photograph Archive/Alamy Stock Photo; p. 116 Epics/Hulton Archive/Getty Images; p. 125 © Look and Learn/Illustrated Papers Collection/Bridgeman Images; p. 141 Chronicle/Alamy Stock Photo; p. 153 Jeff J Mitchell/Getty Images; p. 156 Natalia Sidorova/Shutterstock.com.

CONTENTS

The only surviving group portrait of the Brontë sisters, (*left to right*) Anne, Emily, and Charlotte, was painted by their brother, Branwell, when he was a teenager. He had planned to include himself in the portrait but changed his mind, covering up his image with the shadowy column in the center of the portrait.

Early Deaths, Lasting Works: Introducing the Brontë Sisters

April 16, 2016, was a big day for birthdays in the United Kingdom. On the day that marked Queen Elizabeth's ninetieth birthday, however, the country noted the event but did not celebrate it widely. Since 1748, monarchs' official celebrations have been held not on the day of their actual birth but on a Saturday in June. Why? Because the unreliable weather of England is likelier to be fine during the summer. So, on Saturday, June 11, 2016—the queen's *official* birthday—Her Majesty and other members of the royal family, along with more than fourteen hundred military participants and over four hundred musicians, took part in the so-called Trooping the Colour parade, from Buckingham Palace and back again.[1]

On the queen's *actual* birthday in April, however, a major birthday celebration, long in the planning, began to unfold early in the morning in Haworth (pronounced HOW worth), a village in West Yorkshire, a little over 200 miles (322 kilometers)north of London. This was not a celebration in honor of the ninetieth birthday of a living woman with many admirers but rather of the two hundredth birthday of a woman long dead. That person was not the queen but rather another female icon—one might even say literary royalty—revered both in her native land and throughout the world: the nineteenth-century novelist Charlotte Brontë.

The crowds queuing up that morning at the Brontë Parsonage Museum—formerly the home of the Reverend Patrick Brontë and his children—even exceeded those of a normal day.[2] Almost every day of every year, busloads and carloads of tourists arrive from as far away as India, Australia, and Japan, and recently published guides to the museum include ones in languages from Chinese to Urdu. Many visitors to Haworth are fans of the two most famous books to emerge from the confines of the parsonage—Charlotte Brontë's *Jane Eyre* and Emily Brontë's *Wuthering Heights*—or at least of the film or television versions of those novels. Others are familiar with the family's entire literary output, consisting of poems and seven novels. Some are no less intrigued by the lives, tinged in sadness, of the four talented Brontë siblings, who grew up, sickened, and (in all but one case) died in Haworth. All of the siblings suffered episodes of depression. One was an alcoholic and drug addict. None of them reached age forty.

The celebration in honor of Charlotte's two hundredth birthday launched a five-year program to celebrate the bicentenaries of those siblings: brother Branwell's in 2017, Emily's in 2018, and Anne's in 2020. The Brontë Society, which runs the museum, included in its half-decade-long special celebration the year 2019, the two hundredth anniversary of the invitation to the Reverend Patrick Brontë to take up the role of parson in Haworth.[3]

On the main route between Yorkshire and Lancashire, Haworth in the Brontës' day was hardly off the beaten path. If not for the lasting appeal of the sisters' passionate and intense novels, however, the town would not remain a mecca for twenty-first-century literary pilgrims. As one such tourist remarked, what draws many to the parsonage is the unusual fact that each Brontë who lived there was an author: "They all wrote: if it had only been one it would have been different."[4]

Aspiring Authors and Their Focus on Birthdays

As it happens, carefully noting family birthdays was a habit of the Brontë siblings themselves. In their parsonage home in their twenties, the Brontë sisters developed their own version of what today we call a writers' workshop. An 1857 biography of Charlotte, the oldest of the sisters—the first of many biographies devoted to this talented if doomed family—describes the workshop routine: "The sisters retained their old habit . . . of putting away their work at nine o'clock, and beginning their study, pacing up and down the sitting room. At this time, they talked over the stories they were engaged upon, and described their plots. Once or twice a week, each read to the others what she had written, and heard what they had to say about it." Even though none of the sisters seems to have revised her work based on comments from the others, "the readings were of great and stirring interest to all, taking them out of the gnawing pressure of daily-recurring cares, and setting them in a free place."[5] Their father was aware that his daughters engaged in these exchanges but thought it best not to intrude on them. He later wrote,

> When my daughters were at home they read their manuscripts to each other and gave their candid opinions of what was written. I never interfer'd with them at these times—I judged it best to throw them upon their own responsibility—Besides, a clergyman, bordering upon the age of eighty years, was likely to be too cold and severe a critic of the efforts of buoyant and youthful genius.[6]

In the parsonage, the two younger sisters, Emily and Anne, developed another habit, the writing of "Diary Papers" or "Birthday Notes." Every three or four years, from at least 1834 to 1845, often on the eve or the day of a family member's birthday, Emily and Anne would write brief reports about current events in the parsonage and the world beyond, developments in the imaginary world about which the sisters wrote, and hopes about the future. Emily was sixteen and Anne fourteen when they collaborated on the first of these notes to survive to the present day, written on November 24, 1834. Emily concludes this diary note by wondering "what we shall be like and what we shall be and where we shall be, if all goes on well, in the year 1874—in which year I shall be in my 57th year. Anne will be in her 55th year Branwell will be going in his 58th year and Charlotte in her 59th year Hoping we shall all be well at that time."[7] Emily and Anne could not have known that all of the siblings would be long dead by 1874.

Anne and Emily cosigned that diary note but wrote independent notes in late July 1845, when Emily turned twenty-seven. Anne's note makes clear the sisters used the notes as a type of personal time capsule, to be put away for examination on the same date several years later: "I wonder how we shall all be and where and how situated <when we open this pap> on the thirtyeth of July 1848 when if we are all alive Emily will be just <thirty> '30' I shall be in my 29th year Charlotte in her 33rd and Branwell in his 32nd and what changes shall we have seen and known and shall we be much chan[g]ed ourselves?"[8] (The words in brackets are words that Anne crossed out.)

A year before the 1845 diary paper's projected date of July 30, 1848, the three sisters were months away from publishing the novels that brought them fame. A month before the projected date, Anne's second novel was published. Before the end of 1848, however, Branwell and Emily were both dead, and Anne died the following May. By 1855, Charlotte had also died. Admirers of the Brontë sisters, wondering what they might have achieved had they lived longer, can only agree with Charlotte's widower, the Reverend Arthur Bell Nicholls, who remarked about the diary papers, "They are sad reading poor girls!"[9]

The Brontë sisters may have had short lives, but their literary legacy lives on. More than 150 years after their deaths, for example, a survey of English readers selected two books

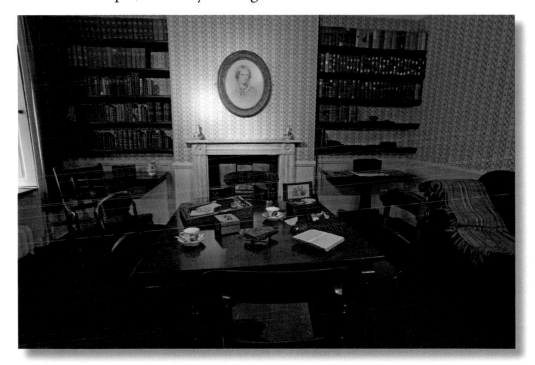

Despite some sources claiming that the sisters' "writers' workshop" met in the sitting room, the Brontë Parsonage Museum explains that the girls held their workshop meetings here in the dining room: "Charlotte, Emily and Anne did most of their writing here and the room was the focus of their creativity. *Jane Eyre, Wuthering Heights* and *Agnes Grey* were written in this room."

that emerged from the parsonage workshop as among the top twenty love stories of all time. Emily Brontë's *Wuthering Heights* topped the list, while Charlotte Brontë's *Jane Eyre* rated number four. "It's really heartening to see how these stories, written so long ago, retain the power to captivate 21st-century audiences," said a representative of the television channel that commissioned the study.[10]

How the Brontë Sisters Helped Shape the History of the Novel

Today it is generally agreed that the author of the first English novel, which appeared 159 years before the Brontës' first novels, was also a woman. Aphra Behn, who lived from 1640 to 1689 (and thus was older at the time of her early death than any of the Brontë siblings), was the first Englishwoman to earn her living through writing. Her novel *Oroonoko*, published the year before her death, was the story of an enslaved African prince. Until feminist criticism began to be written in the last decades of the twentieth century, however, it was more common to call Daniel Defoe's 1719 *Robinson Crusoe* the first English novel. Aware of the tendency to dismiss or undervalue the work of women writers, the Brontë sisters chose to publish under pen names that left the matter of their gender unclear. As Charlotte explained in 1850,

> We veiled our own names under those of Currer, Ellis, and Acton Bell; the ambiguous choice being dictated by a sort of conscientious scruple at assuming Christian names positively masculine, while we did not like to declare ourselves women, because—without at that time suspecting that our mode of writing and thinking was not what is called "feminine"—we had a vague impres-

sion that authoresses are liable to be looked on with prejudice.[11]

During the century and a half years between Behn's *Oroonoko* and the publication of *Jane Eyre, Wuthering Heights*, and *Agnes Grey* (Anne Brontë's first novel), other writers developed different forms of the novel. Each of the Brontë sisters was influenced by and made some use of these older novelistic forms, including the epistolary novel (told through letters); the Gothic novel (characterized by horror, violence, and supernatural effects and usually set against a background of a gloomy and isolated castle); the domestic novel (which examines the home and family); the "condition of England" novel (which analyzes the social upheavals that followed the Industrial Revolution, during which, from about 1760 on in England, power-driven machinery replaced hand tools); and the bildungsroman (German for "novel of education," which describes the personal development of an individual from youth on).

epistolary novel

A novel whose story is told through letters.

Gothic novel

A novel characterized by horror, violence, and supernatural effects, usually set against a background of a gloomy and isolated castle.

domestic novel

A novel that examines the home and family.

Each sister, however, found her own distinctive voice and made her own contribution to the novel. As Charlotte wrote to her editor W. S. Williams, the whole point of being a writer was to be unlike those who came before her:

The standard heroes and heroines of novels, are personages in whom I could never, from childhood upwards, take an interest, believe to be natural, or wish to imitate: were I obliged to copy these characters, I would simply— not write at all. Were I obliged to copy any former novelist, even the greatest, . . . in anything, I would not write—Unless I have something of my own to say, and a way of my own to say it in, I have no business to publish; unless I can look beyond the greatest Masters, and study Nature herself, I have no right to paint; unless I can have the courage to use the language of Truth in preference to the jargon of Conventionality I ought to be silent.[12]

Each sister wrote a novel that challenged the ideas of the day on what was fit to print. In their pursuit of what seemed to them the Truth, the Brontë sisters were willing to accept the verdict of some reviewers that their novels were "coarse." Charlotte's *Jane Eyre* explores, among other things, a young woman's sexual passion. Emily's *Wuthering Heights* gives graphic descriptions of domestic brutality. Anne's second novel, *The Tenant of Wildfell Hall*, depicts a husband's alcoholism and debauchery. In another letter to her editor, Charlotte spoke only for herself but might have been speaking for her sisters as well when she insisted on the importance of capturing both "Passion" and "Feelings" in fictional accounts of life. The Brontë sisters, each in her own way, conveyed "what throbs fast and full, though hidden, what the blood rushes through, what is the unseen seat of Life and the sentient target of Death"—precisely those things that Charlotte found lacking in the work of their famous predecessor, novelist Jane Austen.[13] In

bildungsroman

A "novel of education," which describes the personal development of the main character.

Charlotte's estimation, Jane Austen, though a master of the novel of manners (a type of novel that realistically depicts the customs, behaviors, habits, and expectations of a social group), failed to convey the passions underlying the inner conflicts of her characters.

novel of manners

A novel that realistically depicts the customs, behaviors, habits, and expectations of a social group.

The Brontës made a number of other contributions to the novel. Charlotte's *Jane Eyre* has been called the first bildungs-

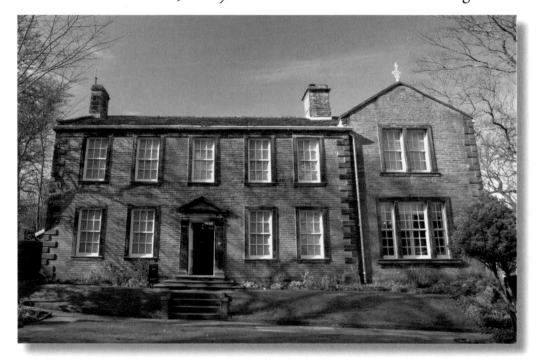

This, the Brontë Parsonage, became the family home in 1820, when Patrick Brontë was appointed curate of St. Michael's and All Angels' Church in Haworth. The Reverend Brontë lived there for forty-four years, though all of his children predeceased him. In 1928, it opened as a museum to honor the lives and works of the Brontë sisters.

roman to focus on the education and development of a female child and the first novel to examine the thoughts and motivations of a young girl. Emily's *Wuthering Heights*, considered unique in English literature, is a powerful work that uses traditional literary forms but nonetheless manages to overturn the conventions of the novel. It somehow combines a realistic representation of speech and character in the north of England while rejecting conventional reality. It has been called the only novel to approach the intensity, scope, and power of a Shakespearean tragedy. Though Anne's novels are not as famous as her sisters', recent feminist criticism has shown that they are worthy of study in their own right. Among other things, their unflinching assessment of how society's expectations cripple not only women but also men is appreciated today.

BRONTË PARSONAGE MUSEUM

After the family died out with the death of Patrick Brontë in 1861, keepsakes and letters in the possession of employees and friends were auctioned off. Some thirty years later, the Brontë Society was formed and began to collect what became known as "Brontëana," which constitutes anything to do with the family, including but not limited to letters, diary papers, clothing, artwork, combs, and furniture. The first museum to display the collection was in a bank in Haworth, which attracted around ten thousand visitors in its first year. In 1928, Yorkshire industrialist and businessman Sir James Roberts bought Haworth Parsonage, set it up as a museum, and presented it to the Brontë Society. In 2011, Charlotte's mahogany desk was donated anonymously, an example of how the collection has continued to grow over the decades.[15]

Enduring Appeal

In the sisters' diary paper of June 1837, written on the eve of their brother Branwell's twentieth birthday, Emily notes that "Queen Victoria ascended the throne this month."[14] The queen, who was only eighteen at the time of her coronation, went on to reign for sixty-four years. Today the term "Victorian" often refers to the prudishness and adherence to social convention that are considered characteristics of Victoria's long reign. Twenty-first-century readers have very different expectations from their reading material than did the Victorian readers of the Brontës' time. That *Jane Eyre* remains a beloved novel and *Wuthering Heights* an admired one today is due at least in part to the passionate intensity of their authors' writing. Even readers who have been through the sisters' best-known novels only once are likely to have indelibly printed on their memories such lines as "Reader, I married him,"[16] "Nelly, I am Heathcliff,"[17] and "I can not live without my life! I can not live without my soul!"[18]

Another reason the Brontës' novels are still read and reread today is that their themes remain alive and fresh. Twenty-first-century readers continue to be engaged by such issues as the vulnerability of children, the role of education in civilizing members of society, the mysteries of love, and women's independence or lack thereof. In short, these books convey basic truths about the human experience that are as meaningful in our day as they were in the mid-nineteenth century. Like other classic works of literature, the Brontës' novels offer details and observations

---

Victorian

A term used to refer to traits associated with English society during the long reign of Queen Victoria (1837–1901), including prudishness and conventionality.

that first-time readers, eager to get on with the plot, might not notice initially but that present them with new layers to discover and unfold with each rereading. Shelves of works about these novels have already been published and continue to appear every year, demonstrating that close readings of *Jane Eyre* and *Wuthering Heights* can still yield new and illuminating interpretations. The Brontës' lives may have been short, but the works they crafted in their Yorkshire parsonage home have proven their enduring appeal. First-time readers of the Brontës can look forward to a literary treat. Those already familiar with the works can expect to appreciate what the novels continue to reveal each time they are approached anew. By paying careful attention to the different devices the sisters employ, you, too, can interpret the Brontës' novels for yourself with confidence.

An Incubator for Authors: The Seeds of the Brontë Sisters' Earliest Work

Single-parent families in twenty-first-century America are hardly unusual. Some population experts believe that half of all children will live with a single mother at some time before they turn eighteen.[1] At the same time, men make up a growing share of American single-parent households.[2] In nineteenth-century England, however, the Brontë sisters' situation was an uncommon one. Left motherless at an early age, the children were raised primarily by their father, with the assistance of an aunt and female employees. Like many single parents, Reverend Patrick Brontë doubtless felt, at least on occasion, not quite up to the task. In the last years of his life, however, he seems to have realized how appropriate his style of fathering was in nurturing the gifts of his prodigiously talented children.

On July 30, 1857, this father who outlived all his children wrote Elizabeth Gaskell, Charlotte's friend and first biographer. He asked her to tone down some of her descriptions of his supposedly eccentric behavior in the next edition of *The Life of Charlotte Brontë*: "I do not deny that I am somewhat eccentrick [sic]. Had I been numbered amongst the calm, sedate, concentric men of the world, I should not have been as I now am, and I should, in all probability, never have had such

19

The Reverend Patrick Brontë, father of three daughters who grew up to be published poets and novelists, was himself the author of several volumes of poems and short tales. The son of a farm laborer, he went on to earn a BA in theology from St. John's College, Cambridge.

children as mine have been."[3] In fact, without a father like
Patrick, the Brontë siblings might very well not have developed into an extraordinary literary family.

Two years earlier, when Gaskell had begun to assemble
material to write her biography of Charlotte, Patrick sent her
two letters. The first letter indicates that not only the siblings'
father but also their grandfather, Hugh Prunty (or Brunty),
was quite a remarkable man. Though Hugh was a poor
Irish farmer, "he and my mother, by dint of application and
industry, managed to bring up a family of ten children in a
respectable manner."[4] Hugh was a well-known storyteller and
ballad singer, who could terrify his listeners with tales drawn
from Irish legend or family history, making it impossible for
them to sleep that night. His granddaughters never knew
Hugh, but their father carried on the family storytelling tradition during meals in the parsonage.

Hugh taught his children to read the Bible and the works
of important English authors, including John Milton and John
Bunyan. His granddaughters would later immerse themselves
in Milton's epic poem *Paradise Lost* (1667) and Bunyan's prose
allegory, *Pilgrim's Progress* (Part I, 1678; Part II, 1684). In a
prose allegory, characters, objects, incidents, and descriptions have not only an apparent, literal meaning, but other
meanings as well. In *Pilgrim's Progress*, for example, the hero,
Christian, stands for all Christian souls, and the difficulties
he encounters on his journey to the Heavenly City represent
the perils Christians face during their earthly existence. Christian's journey is also known as a spiritual pilgrimage—a search
for a personal relationship with God.

Patrick's extraordinary educational gifts led him to achieve
several goals against all odds. By the age of sixteen, he had
established his own school—one where girls and boys were

epic poem

A very long poem that recounts the adventures of a central heroic figure.

allegory

A literary form wherein characters, objects, incidents, and descriptions have both literal and figurative meanings.

treated equally. In his early twenties, he became a tutor in the family of an important evangelical cleric. Evangelical Christians of the day formed a distinct group within the Church of England. Like other evangelicals, Patrick was more concerned with social problems than with ritual, and he emphasized the authority of the Bible and the importance of a personal relationship with God. Assisted by his employer, Patrick went on at twenty-five to the University of Cambridge, where his fellow students came mostly from wealthy families. There he changed the spelling of the family name to Bronte (pronounced Bronteh), perhaps out of admiration for his military hero, Horatio, Viscount Nelson, who was named Duke of Bronte (a place in Sicily) in 1799. Patrick earned his Cambridge degree shortly after turning twenty-nine. At the age of thirty, he was ordained in the Church of England. Eight years later, *The Cottage in the Wood*, a story and four poems written by Patrick, was published. On the title page, seemingly in error, the printer added the familiar two dots over the "e" in Patrick's last name (called an umlaut), resulting in the spelling that is now famous.

Two years before the publication of this book, Patrick married Maria Branwell. Several years younger than Patrick, Maria came from a comfortable middle-class home in the southwestern English seaport town of Penzance. The couple met in 1812 at the Yorkshire school of Maria's uncle. Maria had come there to help her aunt, and Patrick had been invited to administer exams to the school's pupils of Latin and Greek. While courting, the couple exchanged several letters, in one of which Maria teases her "dear saucy Pat."[5] She was also author of an essay, published many years after her death, called "The Advantages of Poverty in Religious Concerns."

Between April 1814, when their first child was born—a daughter named Maria after her mother—and 1820, when their fifth daughter and last child, Anne, was born, the Reverend and Mrs. Brontë became the parents of six children in rapid succession. All the children were born in the county of Yorkshire: Maria and Elizabeth (born 1815) in Hightown, near the village of Hartshead, where Patrick served as curate; and Charlotte (born 1816), Branwell (born 1817), Emily (born 1818), and Anne (born 1820) in Thornton, where Patrick served as curate before moving to Haworth later in 1820. (Curates serve as assistants to rectors or vicars, as parish priests in the Church of England are called.)

Rebounding from a Terrible Loss

In 1821, Maria Branwell Brontë died from what was probably cancer. Nearly thirty years later, in 1850, Patrick gave his sole surviving child, Charlotte, by now a famous author, a "little packet" of her mother's letters, yellowed with age. In a letter to her friend Ellen Nussey, Charlotte wrote, "it was strange to peruse now for the first time the records of a mind whence my own sprang—and most strange—and at once sad and sweet to find that mind of a truly fine, pure and elevated order. They were written to papa before they were married—there is a rectitude, a refinement, a constancy, a modesty, a sense—a gentleness about them indescribable. I wished She had lived and that I had known her."[6]

During Mrs. Brontë's illness, her older sister, Elizabeth Branwell, had come from Penzance to Haworth to help out at the parsonage. She agreed to stay on after Maria's death. Aunt Branwell, as she was called, never married. Nor did Patrick ever remarry, though he seems to have made a few early awkward attempts to do so. According to Ellen Nussey, who first visited Haworth in the summer of 1833, "Miss Branwell was a very small antiquated little lady," who not only read aloud to her brother-in-law, whose sight was impaired, but also engaged in "lively and intelligent" conversation with him, "and tilted argument without fear against Mr. Brontë."[7] Although the Brontë sisters grew up without witnessing their mother's spunky interactions with their father, Aunt Branwell seems to have served as a fine replacement, providing a role model for the independent and forthright female characters they would later create.

Aunt Branwell helped Patrick with the children's education. According to Charlotte's biographer Elizabeth Gaskell, "I do not know whether Miss Branwell taught her nieces anything besides sewing and the household arts . . . . Their regular lessons were said to their father; and they were always in the habit of picking up an immense amount of miscellaneous information for themselves."[8] If the orphaned girls did not come to love their aunt as a mother, Gaskell asserts that they "had that sort of affection for her which is generated by esteem."[9] Anne, who was not even two when her mother died, shared a room with her aunt, while her older sisters bunked in a different room. Branwell, the only boy, came closest to loving their surrogate mother. In the autumn of 1842, as Aunt Branwell lay dying, Branwell wrote to a friend: "now I am attending at the death-bed of my aunt, who has been for twenty years as my mother." On the day she died, Branwell

According to Elizabeth Gaskell, Charlotte's first biographer, the servants called this little room in the parsonage not a nursery but rather "the children's study." Shown here with a cot used by the Brontë sisters, the room served as the literary and theatrical headquarters of the siblings—the place where they worked on their small magazines and books and where they mounted their dramatic productions.

wrote the same friend, "I have now lost the guide and director of all the happy days connected with my childhood."[10]

In 1824, another addition to the parsonage helped fill the gaping hole left by Maria's untimely death. The Reverend Brontë hired fifty-three-year-old Tabitha Aykroyd as a servant. "Tabby," who died of cholera a little more than a month before Charlotte's death, was nursed through several earlier illnesses by the Brontë sisters. According to Gaskell, Tabby's "own mother could not have had more thought for her nor Miss Brontë had."[11] Emily playfully mimicked Tabby's Yorkshire dialect in the diary paper of 1834, quoting her instructing Anne to "pilloputate" (peel a potato).[12] Listening carefully to Tabby's regional dialect doubtless prepared Emily to render the speech of Joseph, the hypocritical old servant in *Wuthering Heights*.

Suffering and Rebounding from a Second Loss

The five younger Brontë children looked up to their oldest sister, Maria, as something of a surrogate mother. Ellen Nussey later recalled how her friend Charlotte "described Maria as a little mother among the rest, superhuman in goodness and cleverness."[13] According to Gaskell, Maria interested the younger children in the outside world: "Maria read the newspapers, and reported intelligence to her younger sisters which it is wonderful they could take an interest in."[14] Those newspaper stories sparked imaginative games. Family servant Sarah Garrs described these games under Maria's guidance: "Their fun knew no bounds . . . They enjoyed a game of romps, and played with zest."[15]

Although in the first half of the nineteenth century home-schooling for girls was the norm, in December 1823 an advertisement for a new school appeared in the *Leeds Intel-*

ligencer, one of several local newspapers read regularly in the parsonage. Located in Cowan Bridge, a town 45 miles (72 km) from Haworth, the Clergy Daughters' School was open to daughters of all clergymen but especially for "the really necessitous Clergy," as the advertisement noted.[16] The Reverend Brontë had no independent means. Even his house belonged to the church, and if something should happen to him, his children would be homeless orphans. He was prepared to educate his son, Branwell, on his own, to help him prepare for a career. For his daughters, however, the Clergy Daughters' School seemed to be the answer. For an extra fee, the school promised to provide "a more liberal Education . . . for any who may be sent to be educated as Teachers and Governesses."[17]

In 1824 Patrick, with high hopes, sent his four oldest daughters off to Cowan Bridge. Sadly, his hopes were dashed. In June 1855 he briefly summarized the unexpected and unwished-for outcome in a letter to Elizabeth Gaskell: "At the school there, Maria and Elizabeth contracted a consumption, and came home, where they died within six weeks of each other, Maria in the eleventh, and Elizabeth in the tenth year of their age."[18] By the time Charlotte and Emily were withdrawn from the school, Maria was already dead. Elizabeth died two weeks later. The motherless children and orphans depicted in all of Charlotte's novels and in Emily's *Wuthering Heights* reflect the various losses the Brontë children experienced in childhood.

Charlotte's resentment toward the school famously found its way into *Jane Eyre*, where she based Jane's suffering at Lowood School on her family's experiences at Cowan Bridge. Generations of readers have been moved by her vivid descriptions of the strict discipline, the sadistic teachers, the inedible food, and the death of the saintly Helen Burns (modeled, according to Charlotte, on her sister Maria).

In 1848, twenty-three years after the Brontës left the Clergy Daughters' School, Charlotte was able to write a much more objective assessment of the place than the one she conveyed through a child's eyes in *Jane Eyre*:

> My personal knowledge of that institution is very much out of date, being derived from the experience of twenty years ago; the establishment was at that time in its infancy, and a sad ricketty infancy it was. Typhus fever decimated the school periodically, and consumption and scrofula in every variety of form, bad air and water, and bad and insufficient diet can generate, preyed on the ill-fated pupils . . . . But, I understand, it is very much altered for the better since those days. The school is removed from Cowen [sic] Bridge (a situation as unhealthy as it was picturesque, low, damp, beautiful with wood and water) to Casterton: the accommodations, the diet, the discipline, the system of tuition, all are, I believe, entirely altered and greatly improved.[19]

Charlotte, who had always been one of the "little ones," now assumed the mantle of oldest child. With time the family once again recovered, and the children's high spirits returned. Charlotte often thought of her dead sisters, with whom she had had a longer relationship than with her mother. Charlotte's friend Mary Taylor wrote Elizabeth Gaskell in 1856, "She used to speak of her two elder sisters, Maria and Elizabeth, who died at Cowan Bridge. I used to believe them to have been wonders of talent and kindness."[20]

For the next five and a half years, Patrick took charge of his children's education. He gave them access to all the books in his library and to the newspapers he read. Despite his limited means, he provided the children with music lessons and art lessons. The children also had access to Aunt Branwell's books and to the magazines she read, including old copies of the monthly *Lady's Magazine*, which was filled with poetry, short stories, and Gothic romances. In 1840, Charlotte confessed in a letter, "I read them as a treat on holiday afternoons or by stealth when I should have been minding my lessons—I shall never see anything which will interest me so much again." *Lady's Magazine* appears to have been the only reading the Reverend Brontë censored, for in the same letter Charlotte reports, "One black day my father burnt them because they contained foolish love-stories." [21]

Of all the books and period-icals the Brontë children read, however, the one most responsible for turning them into writers was *Blackwood's Edinburgh Magazine.* The family did not have a subscrip

juvenilia
Writings produced during childhood.

tion to *Blackwood's* but borrowed copies dating back to 1818 as well as current issues. *Blackwood's* served as a model for the Brontës' juvenilia, the term generally used for writings produced during childhood. In 1829, first Branwell and then Charlotte "published" a regular magazine called, first, *Branwell's Blackwood's Magazine*, and then, under its new editor, *Blackwood's Young Men's Magazine.*

The Glass Town Federation: Sibling Partnership and Sibling Rivalry

The Brontë juvenilia were launched about a year after the deaths of Maria and Elizabeth. In June 1826, the Reverend Brontë returned from a church conference bearing gifts of a dozen wooden toy soldiers for Branwell, a dancing doll for Anne, a toy village for Emily, and a set of ninepins for Charlotte. Three years later, in her "History of the Year 1829," Charlotte explained how the toy soldiers immediately turned the children into budding playwrights, who wrote and produced that very month the "Young Men's Play":

> Papa bought Branwell some wooden soldiers at Leeds; when papa came home it was night, and we were in bed, so next morning Branwell came to our door with a box of soldiers. Emily and I jumped out of bed, and I snatched up one and exclaimed, "This is the Duke of Wellington! This shall be the Duke!" When I had said

This map of the imaginary country of Angria, drawn by Branwell no later than May 8, 1831, has a prototype—a map of real explorations in northern and central Africa in 1822–1824. The source of the hand-drawn map, the siblings' manuscript *The History of the Young Men from Their First Settlement to the Present Time*, foreshadows what would later become the established genre of alternative histories.

AN EXCERPT FROM THE GLASS TOWN SAGA

"When it was 8 o'clock in the evening, I was sent for to
Captain T———. I found him in his library. He ordered me to
prepare in all haste for a journey to the Glass Town, where he
was to go to attend a funeral that would take place there at
midnight. I thought that an uncommon time for an honest
man to be buried & my curiosity quickened me. In half an
hour all was ready. We set off (for I went with him) & arrived
at the city before eleven. He got out of his carriage at the
Fetish Inn & there he left it with all his servants except me,
whom he ordered to accompany him."
—From *An Interesting Passage in the Lives of Some Eminent
Men of the Present Time, by Lord Charles Wellesley—June the 18
1830, by Charlotte Brontë*[22]

this Emily likewise took up one and said it should be
hers; when Anne came down she said one should be
hers. Mine was the prettiest of the whole, and the tallest,
and the most perfect in every part. Emily's was a grave-
looking fellow, and we called him "Gravey." Anne's was
a queer little thing, much like herself, and we called
him "Waiting-boy." Branwell chose his and called him
"Buonaparte."[23]

In choosing their soldiers' names, Charlotte and Branwell
were clearly engaging in sibling rivalry. The two great polit-
ical rivals of recent times were Britain's Duke of Wellington
and the French military leader Napoleon Bonaparte. In 1815
at the Battle of Waterloo, Wellington had defeated Napoleon,
destroying his plan to rule Europe. The rivalry between Charlotte and Branwell continued throughout their collaboration.
The delight they took in their literary competition is apparent

in the humorous reviews of each other's work they "published" in their own publications using different pen names.

Even though Branwell sometimes called his soldier "Sneaky," the younger girls soon replaced the childish names they had first chosen for their soldiers with those of two Arctic explorers, Parry and Ross, about whose expeditions they had read in *Blackwood's Magazine*. Branwell and Charlotte initiated a series of games involving the "Young Men"—the four children's soldier heroes. They wrote and performed plays based on their heroes' exploits in fictional kingdoms in West Africa. Since the capital city of each kingdom was called Glass Town, the complicated saga that emerged from the siblings' fertile imaginations is often called the Glass Town saga. Feeling relegated to minor roles in the management of the "Young Men" enterprise, however, Emily and Anne eventually "seceded" from the all-sibling effort and formed their own imaginary world of Gondal. The monarch of their imaginary island in the North Pacific was a woman. While Emily and Anne were true collaborators in the development of Gondal, Charlotte and Branwell were both collaborators and competitors in their own, separate, imaginary world, called Angria.

A striking feature of the Brontë juvenilia is the tiny script in which the children wrote their stories, which they bound into tiny hand-sewn booklets. Perhaps the small print was meant to keep their writing on the scale of the toy soldiers who inspired their imaginary worlds. It is also possible the children decided to write this way in order to shield their work from the eyes of prying adults. Since few people can read the writing without a magnifying glass, they probably succeeded in that goal. Confident that their work would not reach adult eyes, the children felt free to write about sexual relationships and evil deeds of which an adult audience would have disapproved.

The Brontës continued to produce the works referred to as juvenilia well into their twenties. Emily remained passionately involved with Gondal until at least 1845. For Charlotte,

This example of the tiny writing used by the Brontë children is the Lord's Prayer, written by Charlotte in 1835. She enclosed the verses from the New Testament book of Matthew within a circle smaller than a dime. Perhaps the prayer was meant to serve as a talisman for one of the toy soldiers who were the inspiration for the characters in the Brontë juvenilia.

AN EXCERPT FROM "ROSINA"

One of Emily's regular characters in the Gondal writings was a princess named Rosina.

> Angora's hills have heard their tread
> The crimson flag is planted there—
> Elderno's waves are rolling red,
> While *I* lie fettered here?
>
> "Nay, rather, Gondal's shaken throne
> Is now secure and free;
> And my King Julius reigns alone,
> Debtless, alas, to me![24]

Angria remained an obsession until late 1839. One of her heroes, Zamorna, eventually replaced Wellington as her favorite character. Zamorna's complex personality and racy personal life would eventually help her shape Rochester, the hero of *Jane Eyre*. Branwell and Anne may have tired sooner of Angria and Gondal, but all four Brontë siblings gained much preprofessional writing experience by creating the sagas of these imaginary worlds. Even though much of the juvenilia of Emily and Anne has never been found, the total number of words in the Brontë juvenilia far exceeds that in all the novels and poems they would eventually publish.

Charlotte as a Teacher in Training

In the summer of 1830, the Reverend Patrick Brontë, now fifty-three years old, became very ill. His brush with death reminded him that his children still lacked the skills to support themselves. He decided to send fourteen-year-old Charlotte off to school. Upon her return, the plan was for her first to train her sisters and then to find a position as a governess or teacher. Patrick continued to educate Branwell at home, giving him a strong background in Latin and Greek, while Aunt Branwell continued her contributions to Emily's and Anne's upbringing.

From January 1831 until July 1832, Charlotte studied at Margaret Wooler's school in Roe Head, about 20 miles (32 km) from Haworth. In her biography of Charlotte, Gaskell reports that "Charlotte Brontë was happy in the choice made for her of the second school to which she was sent."[25] Her happiness was not immediate, however. At Roe Head, where there were

CHARLOTTE MOVES ON

In 1839, Charlotte decided it was time to leave the imaginary world of her childhood behind. She wrote of the painful choice in her manuscript, "Farewell to Angria," an excerpt of which follows:

"I have now written a great many books, & for a long time I have dwelt on the same characters & scenes & subjects... But we must change, for the eye is tired of the picture so oft recurring & now so familiar.

Yet do not urge me too fast reader—it is no easy thing to dismiss from my imagination the images which have filled it so long. They were my friends & my intimate acquaintance & I could with little labour describe to you the faces, the voices, the actions, of those who people my thoughts by day & not seldom stole strangely even into my dreams by night. When I depart from these I feel almost as if I stood on the threshold of a home & were bidding farewell to its inmates...Still, I long to quit for a while that burning clime where we have sojourned too long...."[26]

only ten students, Charlotte made two friends for life, Ellen Nussey and Mary Taylor. Years later, each one recalled Charlotte's difficult first days after five years spent only in the company of her family. Ellen Nussey remembered finding "a silent, weeping, dark little figure in the large bay-window" of one of the schoolrooms. "She did not shrink . . . when spoken to, but in very few words confessed she was 'home-sick.'"[27] Ellen also remembered that "she always seemed to feel that a deep responsibility rested upon her; that she was an object of expense to those at home, and that she must use every moment to attain the purpose for which she was sent to school, i.e., to fit herself for governess life."[28] Mary remembered seeing Charlotte arrive in "a covered cart, in very old-fashioned clothes, and looking very cold and miserable . . . . She looked a little old woman, so short sighted that she always appeared to be seeing something, and moving her head from side to side to catch a sight of it. She was very shy and nervous . . . . We thought her very ignorant, for she had never learnt grammar at all . . . ."[29] Her eyesight was so bad that she was unable to play ball with the other girls.

Eventually, Charlotte settled in. Her fellow students discovered that, woeful though Charlotte's grammar might be, she knew a great deal about literature and painting, could write poetry and make drawings of much higher quality than they could, and was much more knowledgeable about the politics of the day than they were. Charlotte could also tell tales with as much flair as her father and her grandfather. According to Elizabeth Gaskell, "at night, she was an invaluable story-teller, frightening them almost out of their wits as they lay in bed. On one occasion the effect was such that she was led to scream out aloud, and Miss [Wooler], coming upstairs, found that one of the listeners had been seized with violent palpitations

THE GLASS TOWN FEDERATION: EARLY FAN FICTION AND PRECURSOR TO *GAME OF THRONES*

In 2011, the British Library mounted an exhibition on science fiction, in which the Brontës' handwritten Glass Town saga was prominently displayed. A press release for the exhibit made the provocative claim that, though the Brontës are not usually considered science fiction writers, these juvenilia "are one of the first examples of fan fiction, using favourite characters and settings in the same way as science fiction and fantasy fans now play in the detailed imaginary 'universes' of Star Trek or Harry Potter. While the sense of fantasy is strong, there are teasing examples of what might be called the beginnings of science fiction."[30] Strictly speaking, fan fiction is based on characters from an original work of fiction, written not by the original author but by fans of the work, without authorization from the author. The Brontës' Glass Town saga began not with fictional characters but rather with the siblings using famous figures of the day as the focus of their fictional world. Eventually, however, the siblings populated their world with characters of their own creation. The term *"fan fiction,"* therefore, strictly speaking does not apply here. The Brontë early fiction, however, does conform to another characteristic of fan fiction, which is the writer's assumption that readers come to the work with a shared knowledge of its central figures and events. The four siblings were writing for each other and could be confident that their readers were fully informed about the personalities and events in their fictional worlds.

> **fan fiction**
>
> A piece of writing based on characters from an original work of fiction, written by fans of the original work.

Five years later, an article in *the Independent* suggested that the Glass Town saga can also be considered a forerunner to *Game of Thrones*, replete with sexual intrigue, betrayal, and bloody battles.[31]

in consequence of the excitement produced by Charlotte's story."[32] According to Gaskell, the methods of instruction at Roe Head were exemplary. The girls "did not leave off reading and learning as soon as the compulsory pressure of school was taken away. They had been taught to think, to analyse, to reject, to appreciate."[33]

As planned, when Charlotte returned home in 1832, she became her sisters' teacher. On July 21, 1832, she described for Ellen her daily routine at the parsonage: "In the morning from nine o'clock till half past twelve I instruct my Sisters & draw, then we walk till dinner after dinner I sew till tea-time, and after tea I either read, write, do a little fancy-work or draw, as I pl[eas]e Thus in one delightful, though somewhat monotonous course my life is passed."[34]

Almost exactly three years later, Charlotte wrote Ellen of the changes that were about to disrupt the pleasant routines that had given her much time to work on her juvenilia at home:

> We are all about to divide, break up, separate, Emily is going to school, Branwell is going to London, and I am going . . . to teach in the very school where I was myself taught—. Miss Wooler made me the offer and I preferred it to one or two proposals of Private Governessship which I had before received—I am sad, very sad at the thoughts of leaving home but Duty—Necessity— these are stern mistresses will not be disobeyed.[35]

The separation from home would not be complete, since Emily would be a pupil at Roe Head, where she, too, could get the education needed to teach others. Anne would be alone in the parsonage with her father and aunt, while Charlotte and Branwell would take their first steps on the road to professional careers.

The Gender-Bending Road to Publication: From Reluctant Teachers to Aspiring Authors

Charlotte wrote in 1850 of herself and her siblings, "The liveliest pleasure we had known from childhood upwards, lay in attempts at literary composition."[1] Unfortunately, it was as difficult then to support oneself exclusively as a writer as it is now. Impelled by an innate sense of duty, therefore, the young Brontës tried valiantly but unsuccessfully between 1835 and 1845 to find satisfaction in nonliterary careers that would enable them reliably to make ends meet. Before they were able to launch themselves as authors, they had to endure a difficult decade, marked not only by a series of false starts but also by several bouts of depression.

When Charlotte wrote her friend Ellen in the summer of 1835 that Branwell planned to go to London, she was referring to her brother's decision to pursue a career as a portrait painter. In 1834, he had painted two oil portraits of the Brontë siblings, and he now thought of getting more formal training at the Royal Academy of Arts in London. Probably realizing that he lacked the kind of portfolio the academy required for admission, he never did enroll. Over the next decade, Branwell tried his hand at several different careers. After a brief stint as a portrait painter (1838–1839), he served as a clerk for the Leeds and Manchester Railway (1840–1842) and as a private tutor (1839–1840, 1843–1845). While he left his portrait studio of his own accord, he was dismissed from the other positions.

This group portrait of the Brontë siblings, painted by Branwell in 1833–1834, includes the artist himself, holding a gun. The only part of the painting that still exists is the portrait of Emily on the right. The rest was destroyed sometime after the death of the Reverend Brontë by Charlotte's widower, Arthur Bell Nicholls, who thought the likenesses too poor to save. A daguerreotype of the painting had been made before 1860, however, and an engraving of the original work was made based on it. In 1989, a photograph of the daguerreotype, taken around 1879, was also found.

None of Branwell's attempts to earn a living in nonliterary ways worked out, but he held tight to his hopes of supporting himself through his writing. For a while, he threw himself into writing about Angria, the imaginary kingdom he and Charlotte had created. He also wrote several times to *Blackwood's Magazine*, hoping to be accepted as a regular contributor. Although he developed addictions to both alcohol and opium, Branwell was actually the first of the Brontë siblings to be published. Between 1841 and 1847, he had over a dozen poems published in newspapers. Then, realizing that a novelist could earn more money than a poet, he began to work on a novel.

Emily had the least success in the outside world of work. Charlotte's position as a teacher at Roe Head School was to cover the cost of tuition to train Emily for a career. Emily, however, suffered from depression at school, and she left after only a few months. In 1850 Charlotte described Emily's suffering:

> Liberty was the breath of Emily's nostrils; without it, she perished. The change from her own home to a school, and from her own very noiseless, very secluded, but unrestricted . . . mode of life, to one of disciplined routine . . ., was what she failed in enduring. Her nature proved here too strong for her fortitude. Every morning when she woke, the vision of home and the moors rushed on her, and darkened and saddened the day that lay before her. Nobody knew what ailed her but me—I knew only too well. In this struggle her health was quickly broken: her white face, attenuated form, and failing strength threatened rapid decline. I felt in my heart she would die if she did not go home, and with this conviction obtained her recall.[2]

Back at home, Emily helped with housekeeping, always having a book propped on the kitchen table while she did her chores. She also continued her Gondal writing and enjoyed her long walks on the moors. Despite her experience at Roe Head, Emily tried her hand at teaching for two terms at the Law Hill School. In one of her underpunctuated letters to her friend Ellen, Charlotte correctly predicted the outcome of this attempt: "My Sister Emily is gone into a Situation as a teacher in a large school of near forty pupils near Halifax. I have had one letter from her since her departure . . . it gives an appalling account of her duties—Hard labour from six in the morning until near eleven at night with only one half hour of exercise between—this is slavery [and] I fear she will never stand it—[sic]"[3] At first, Emily was able to turn her homesickness into poems that would eventually become well known. During the second term, however, depression set in, she wrote no poetry, and her health declined. By March 1839 she had returned home.

Of all the sisters, Anne had the most successful teaching career. Nonetheless, like Emily, whom she replaced at Roe Head in the autumn of 1835, Anne also experienced a health crisis there. Hers, however, had a religious component to it. During Anne's illness in late 1837, she was visited by the Reverend James de la Trobe, the clergyman at a nearby chapel. De la Trobe wrote that Anne had suffered from "a severe attack of gastric fever which brought her very low, and her voice was only a whisper; her life hung on a narrow thread."[4] Anne's poetry from that time reflected her feelings of misery and isolation:

> I'm buried now; I've done with life;
> I've done with hate, revenge and strife;

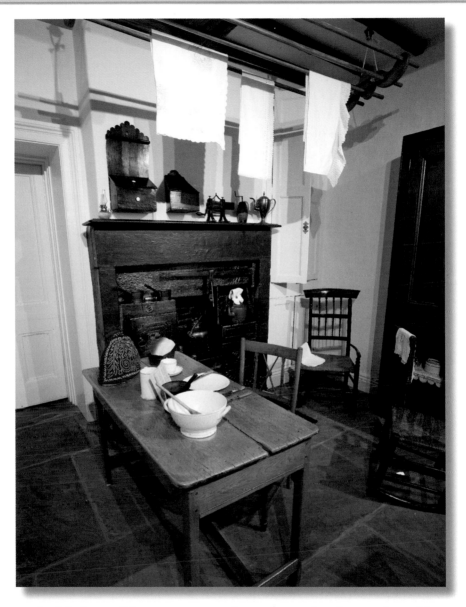

In the kitchen of the parsonage, shown here, the sisters shared in the household work with the servants. While they worked, they were often entertained by their live-in cook-housekeeper Tabitha Aykroyd, known as Tabby, who told tales of the Yorkshire moors. Tabby is believed to have served as the model not only for Nelly Dean in Emily's *Wuthering Heights* but also for the housekeeper Martha in Charlotte's *Shirley*.

I've done with joy, and hope and love
And all the bustling world above.

Long have I dwelt forgotten here
In pining woe and dull despair;
This place of solitude and gloom
Must be my dungeon and my tomb.

No hope, no pleasure can I find:
I am grown weary of my mind;
Often in balmy sleep I try
To gain a rest from misery,

And in one hour of calm repose
To find a respite from my woes,
But dreamless sleep is not for me
And I am still in misery.

(Excerpt from "A Voice from the Dungeon,"
October 1837)[5]

De la Trobe's religious reassurances appear to have helped Anne through her spiritual crisis: "her heart opened to the sweet views of salvation, pardon, and peace in the blood of Christ, and she accepted His welcome to the weary and heavy laden sinner . . . had she died then, I should have counted her His redeemed and ransomed child."[6] The Reverend Brontë, alerted by Miss Wooler, brought both Charlotte and Anne home. By early January 1838, Charlotte was able to report to Ellen, "Anne is now much better—though she still requires a great deal of care—however I am relieved from my worst fears respecting her—"[7]

Once her recuperation was complete, Anne returned to Roe Head for another year. After leaving school, she worked the next six years as a private governess to two families, the

Inghams (1839) and the Robinsons (1840–1845). During these years, she spent at most five or six weeks at home. Eventually, her experiences as a governess would contribute to the plot and texture of her two novels.

Charlotte taught at Miss Wooler's school from late July 1835 until just before Christmas 1838, moving with the school from Roe Head to Dewsbury Moor, some 3 or 4 miles (4.8 to 6.4 km) away, in early 1848. It did not take Charlotte very long to discover that she had no vocation for teaching. Six pieces of a journal that Charlotte kept at Roe Head have survived. They provide proof that Charlotte would much rather have been writing about her imaginary worlds than dealing with live pupils in the real one. On August 11, 1836, for example, she wrote,

> The thought came over me am I to spend all the best part of my life in this wretched bondage, forcibly suppressing my rage at the idleness the apathy and the hyperbolical & most asinine stupidity of these fat-headed oafs and on compulsion assuming an air of kindness, patience & assiduity?

> must I from day to day sit chained to this chair prisoned with in these four bare-walls, while these glorious summer suns are burning in heaven & the year is revolving in its richest glow & declaring at the close of every summer day\the time I am lost/<it> will never come again? . . . Then came on me rushing impetuously . . . I felt as if I could <have> written gloriously—I longed to write . . . if I had <it> had time to indulge it I felt that the vague sensations of that moment would have settled down into some narrative better at least than any thing I ever produced before. But just then a Dolt came up with a lesson. I thought I should have vomited.[8]

Charlotte's sense that her destiny was to be an author led her to contact the poet Robert Southey on December 29, 1836. It must have taken a great deal of courage for a twenty-year-old female teacher to ask the man who had been named poet laureate of England in 1813 to evaluate her literary talents. Charlotte's letter has never been found, but Southey's reply of March 12, 1837, makes clear that she told him about her wish to be "for ever known" as a poetess.[9] While Southey assured her that "you evidently possess & in no inconsiderable degree . . . 'the faculty of Verse,'" he cautioned that "many volumes of poems are now published every year without attracting public attention . . . . Whoever therefore is ambitious of distinction in this way, ought to be prepared for disappointment." He also warned that the "daydreams in which you habitually indulge" would prevent her from fulfilling her duties. To twenty-first-century eyes, several lines in particular stand out from Southey's basically very kind letter : "Literature cannot be the business of a woman's life: & it ought not to be. The more she is engaged in her proper duties, the less leisure will she have for it . . . To those duties you have not yet been called, & when you are you will be less eager for celebrity."[10]

Charlotte's response to Southey reveals the conflict within her between duty and what she saw as her true calling:

> My Father is a clergyman of limited . . . income, and I am the eldest of his children. He expended quite as much in my education as he could afford in justice to the rest. I thought it therefore my duty, when I left school, to become a governess. In that capacity, I find enough to occupy my thoughts all day long . . . without having a moment's time for one dream of the imagination . . . . I have endeavoured not only attentively to observe all the

On March 12, 1837, the poet Robert Southey advised Charlotte,
who had sent him some of her work for feedback, that women
should not aspire to become professional writers. Although
Charlotte saved Southey's response in a wrapper inscribed with
the words "Southey's advice: To be saved forever," she nonetheless
drafted around sixty poems and verse fragments over the months
following her receipt of his response.

47

duties a woman ought to fulfil, but to feel deeply interested in them. I don't always succeed, for sometimes when I'm teaching or sewing I would rather be reading or writing; but I try to deny myself . . . I trust I shall never more feel ambitious to see my name in print; if the wish should arise, I'll look at Southey's letter, and suppress it.[11]

Charlotte may have put aside her literary dreams for the time being, but her health finally broke under the monotony of her daily routine at school. On June 9, 1838, she wrote Ellen, "I ought to be at Dewsbury-Moor you know—but I stayed as long as I was able and at length I neither could nor dared stay any longer. My health and spirits had utterly failed me and the medical man whom I consulted enjoined me if I valued my life to go home. So home I went . . . and I am now I trust fairly in the way to be myself again . . . after weeks of mental and bodily anguish not to be described something like tranquility and ease began to dawn again."[12]

Charlotte did return to Miss Wooler's school, but she finally resigned that December. After spending several months without employment, Charlotte took a temporary position as a governess. Her letter to Emily of June 8, 1839, summarizes her assessment of that profession: "I see now more clearly than I have ever done before that a private governess has no existence, is not considered as a living and rational being except as connected with the wearisome duties she has to fulfil."[13] Nonetheless, as Gaskell notes, "Much as she disliked the life of a private governess, it was her duty to relieve her father of the burden of her support, and this was the only way open to her."[14] In 1841, Charlotte therefore took what would be her final post as a governess, at the home of Mr. and Mrs. John White. "This time she esteemed herself fortunate in becoming a member of a kind-hearted and friendly household."[15] Charlotte's employers, in fact, gave her a new lease on life. They endorsed a plan that the sisters had come up with during the winter of 1839–1840. According to Gaskell, "the favourite idea was that of keeping a school. They thought that . . . a small number of pupils . . . might be accommodated in the parsonage. As teaching seemed the only profession open to them, and as it appeared that Emily at least could not live away from home, while the others also suffered much from the same cause, this plan of school-keeping presented itself as most desirable."[16]

The problem the sisters encountered was that it would take some money to set up a school, and the only person to whom they could turn for a loan was Aunt Branwell. The sisters had been unable to persuade her that this venture would be a good risk. The support of the Whites, however, led Charlotte to write her aunt a persuasive letter that would lead to a momentous change in her life: "Mr. and Mrs. White, and others, . . . recommend me, if I desire to secure permanent success, to delay commencing the school for six months longer, and by all means to contrive, by hook or by crook, to spend the intervening time in some school on the continent. They say schools in England are so numerous, competition so great, that without some such step towards attaining superiority we shall probably have a very hard struggle, and may fail in the end . . . "[17]

Asking for a loan, Charlotte proposed going to Brussels, the capital of Belgium, together with Emily, with a view to improving their language skills. She told her aunt, "I feel an absolute conviction that, if this advantage were allowed us, it would be the making of us for life . . . I look to you, aunt to help us."[18] Her appeal was successful.

Love Unrequited Becomes the Stuff of Novels

From February through November 1842, Charlotte and Emily studied at the Pensionnat Heger, a private school run by Madame Zoë Heger in Brussels. Their main teacher was Madame Heger's husband, Monsieur Constantin Heger. In January 1843 Charlotte returned alone to teach there. The two years in Brussels had an enormous and lasting effect on her. Monsieur Heger's demanding exercises in French composition helped Charlotte not only to improve her French but also to trim her English writing style. Even more importantly, however, for Charlotte's career as a writer, she fell madly but hopelessly in love with him.

While Charlotte benefited from Monsieur Heger's teaching methods, Emily balked at them. He had the sisters read masterpieces of French literature and use them as models for their own compositions on similar subjects. According to Elizabeth Gaskell, "After explaining his plan to them, he awaited their reply. Emily spoke first; and said that she saw no good to be derived from it; and that, by adopting it, they should lose all originality of thought and expression."[19] Charlotte more willingly submitted to Monsieur Heger's regimen. His careful comments on her work helped her outgrow the undisciplined writing of her Angrian tales and learn to control her style as a novelist.

In November 1842 the sad news of Aunt Branwell's death reached the sisters in Brussels. Together, they returned to the parsonage, but only Charlotte traveled back to Brussels in late January 1843. During the course of that year, Charlotte became obsessed with Monsieur Heger. As biographer Helen MacEwan explains, Heger's dramatic teaching methods may have been responsible for Charlotte's enchantment:

> [Monsieur Heger] had a huge love of language and
> literature and could engage with Charlotte and Emily
> intellectually, but equally attractive for Charlotte was
> his personality. Like many inspiring teachers he was
> eccentric and temperamental. The storms that erupted
> when he lost his temper and made his pupils cry for
> failing to live up to his expectations alternated with the
> sunny spells of his more benevolent humours . . . Heger
> had great histrionic talent, and the frequency of tears
> in classes over which he presided was owing to the way
> he worked on his pupils' emotions to make them more
> receptive to the beauties of literature.[20]

Aware of Charlotte's infatuation with her husband, Madame
Heger began to behave coolly toward her. In a letter of May
1843, Charlotte confided that "M. Heger is wonderously influenced by Madame . . . . I fancy he has taken to considering me
as a person to be let alone—and consequently he has in a great
measure withdrawn the light of his countenance."[21]

Feeling terribly isolated in Brussels, Charlotte decided to
return home at the end of 1843. Though Monsieur Heger did
not return Charlotte's love, he thought highly of her accom-
plishments and abilities. According to Gaskell, to advance the
sisters' plan of opening a school of their own, he "gave her a
kind of diploma . . . certifying that she was perfectly capable
of teaching the French language, having well studied the
grammar and composition thereof, and, moreover, having
prepared herself for teaching by studying and practising the
best methods of instruction."[22]

The money Aunt Branwell had left each of her nieces
would, in theory, be able to help them get their school off
the ground. Shortly after Charlotte's return home, the sisters
had an advertisement for "The Misses Brontë's Establishment

for the Board and Education of a Limited Number of Young Ladies" printed. No students signed up, however.

Charlotte had a great deal of difficulty overcoming her infatuation with Monsieur Heger. She sent him letters twice a week until Madame Heger wrote a formal note on her husband's behalf, instructing her to limit her letters to two a year. Four of her letters survive, written primarily in French. In her letter of November 18, 1845, Charlotte admits that his failure to write makes her "feverish," causes her to lose both "appetite and sleep," and leaves her in despair.[23] In a letter to Ellen Nussey after her final return home in January 1844, Charlotte writes, "I suffered much before I left Brussels—I think however long I live I shall not forget what the parting with Monsr Heger cost me."[24] The passionate writing in her novels captures some of her own experience of love and loss. In three of the novels Charlotte would write over the next decade, an essay a student writes for her teacher plays a role in the love that develops between them. What never happened for her in real life she would make happen for the heroines of her fiction.

An "Accidental" Discovery and the Launching of Three Careers

The Brontë sisters' dream of setting up a school of their own was now dead. What about "the dream of one day becoming authors," which they "had very early cherished"?[25]

The summer and autumn of 1845 marked a period of crisis for the Brontës. It was clear that their various attempts at nonliterary careers had failed. All the siblings were at home again. Emily and Charlotte had been living at home since returning from Brussels in 1842 and 1844, respectively. According to Emily's 1845 diary paper, Anne had left her position as governess to the Robinsons "of her own accord."[26] Branwell, too, was no longer employed as a tutor at the Robinsons', where he had joined Anne in 1843. The discovery of Branwell's inappropriate behavior with Mrs. Robinson led to his dismissal in 1845. What would the Brontës do now? Even though the girls had modest inheritances from Aunt Branwell, they would still need to earn a living.

Ironically, though Branwell now became a heavy drinker and user of opiates, he understood that writing was a better way "to wile away my torment." He also was the first of the siblings to grasp that "in the present state of the publishing and reading world a Novel is the most saleable article."[27] He reworked eight-year-old Angrian material in the light of his involvement with Mrs. Robinson. The novel was never finished, but it gave focus to those remaining days of his life when his brain was unclouded by drink or drugs.

Although the sisters continued writing privately, it took them longer than Branwell to figure out that their literary talents were their best resource. In 1850 Charlotte described her role in launching their professional writing careers: "One day, in the autumn of 1845, I accidentally lighted on a MS. volume of verse in my sister Emily's handwriting." ("MS." is an abbreviation for "manuscript." Even though today a "manuscript" submitted to a publisher is usually prepared on a computer, the word actually comes from the Latin words meaning "written by hand." Remember that the typewriter, much less the computer, had yet to be invented, so all the Brontës' works were handwritten until they were set in type to be printed.)

Charlotte's "accidental" discovery has been described as a "moment that changed literary history."[28] It also appears not to have been truly accidental but rather to have resulted from her unauthorized poking around in Emily's private papers, since "it took hours to reconcile her to the discovery I had made, and days to persuade her that such poems merited publication."[29] After overcoming Emily's resistance to the plan, the sisters' childhood literary dream "now suddenly acquired strength and consistency: it took the character of a resolve." With Charlotte playing the role of literary agent, the sisters endured the humiliation of "a string of terse rejection notes."[30] One publisher, however, suggested submitting the manuscript to a press that specialized in poetry. And so, in May 1846, a volume of their poems appeared under their gender-neutral pseudonyms: Acton, Ellis, and Currer Bell. At Charlotte's naïve request, the publisher—Aylott & Jones—issued a print run of one thousand copies. This was an extravagant number at a time when "even established greats like Elizabeth Barrett Browning and William Wordsworth himself were finding it hard to get their work into print and then on to bookshelves."[31]

WHAT BECAME OF THE OTHER VOLUMES OF POETRY BY THE "BELLS"?

To keep the unsold books from being remaindered—liquidated by the publisher at greatly reduced prices or even shredded—Charlotte sent unsolicited copies to well-known writers, including essayist Thomas de Quincey, to whom she wrote in mid-June 1847. But it is a little-known fact that Smith, Elder and Co.—the publisher that agreed to publish *Jane Eyre* only a little over a year later—purchased the remaining 961 books from Aylott and Jones for the sum of 6 pence each. The sisters thus actually earned a royalty of over 24 British pounds on their first publication, and over the years Smith, Elder sold every remaining copy of the book.[32]

trunk-makers, we have decided on distributing as presents a few copies of what we cannot sell me beg to offer you one in acknowledgment of the pleasure and profit we have often and long derived from your works —

I am Sir
Yours very respectfully
Currer Bell.

June 16th /47

T. De Quincey Esqr

On June 16, 1847, Charlotte sent a copy of *Poems by Currer, Ellis, and Acton Bell* to the author of *Confessions of an English Opium-Eater*, Thomas de Quincey. In the enclosed letter (*pictured*), Charlotte—using her pen name, Currer Bell—wrote, "My relatives, Ellis and Acton Bell and myself, heedless of the repeated warning of various respectable publishers, have committed the rash act of publishing a volume of poems."

The volume, simply titled *Poems*, contains roughly twenty poems by each sister. Much of the poetry was influenced by the Glass Town writings, but universal themes of romantic love, religion, and mortality run throughout the work. In "Faith and Despondency," for example, Emily presents a dialogue between a father and his daughter as a means of exploring her own Christian faith and the existence of an afterlife. When the father questions whether he will ever see his departed friends again, the daughter seeks to reassure him:

> . . . But this world's life has much to dread,
> Not so, my Father, with the dead.
> "Oh! not for them, should we despair,
> The grave is drear, but they are not there;
> Their dust is mingled with the sod,
> Their happy souls are gone to God!
> You told me this, and yet you sigh,
> And murmur that your friends must die.
> Ah! my dear father, tell me why?
> For, if your former words were true,
> How useless would such sorrow be;
> As wise, to mourn the seed which grew
> Unnoticed on its parent tree,
> Because it fell in fertile earth,
> And sprang up to a glorious birth—
> Struck deep its root, and lifted high
> Its green boughs, in the breezy sky.
> "But, I'll not fear, I will not weep
> For those whose bodies rest in sleep,—
> I know there is a blessed shore,
> Opening its ports for me, and mine;
> And, gazing Time's wide waters o'er,
> I weary for that land divine,
> Where we were born, where you and I

Shall meet our Dearest, when we die;
From suffering and corruption free,
Restored into the Deity."

(Excerpt from "Faith and Despondency")[33]

Despite the fact that reviews were generally favorable, only two copies were sold of the volume, for whose printing, publication, and advertising the Brontë sisters had to pay themselves. Even before the first reviews appeared, Charlotte asked Aylott & Jones if they would consider publishing "a work of fiction—consisting of three distinct and unconnnected tales" that the "Bells" were working on.[34] Having been advised to try other publishers, Charlotte began to send off their first three novels in early July 1846. There were no immediate takers.

THE BREAKTHROUGH BOOK: CURRER BELL'S JANE EYRE

Jane Eyre, the first of Charlotte's novels to be published, remains her most famous work. It was not, however, the manuscript Charlotte began to circulate in the summer of 1846 along with Emily's *Wuthering Heights* and Anne's *Agnes Grey*. That book, *The Professor*, based on her experiences in Brussels, was not destined to be published in Charlotte's lifetime. On August 25, 1846, the already oft-rejected manuscript of *The Professor* reached Charlotte in Manchester, where her father was undergoing eye surgery for a cataract that had left him virtually blind. According to Gaskell, "Charlotte told me that her tale came back upon her hands, curtly rejected by some publisher, on the very day when her father was to submit to his operation." A less determined person might have given up. Charlotte, however, not only continued to send *The Professor* out to other publishers, but also "in this time of care and depressing inquietude" began to write *Jane Eyre*.[1]

Imagine oldest sister Charlotte's dismay when, in July 1847, after a string of rejection letters, a publisher—Thomas Cautley Newby of London—offered to publish Anne's and Emily's manuscripts, but not Charlotte's *The Professor*. The two younger sisters complied with the publisher's request to remit fifty pounds to cover the costs of production. Newby agreed to return their money once he had sold 250 of the 300 copies he

In 1906, Charlotte's widower, Arthur Bell Nicholls, donated this chalk portrait of his deceased wife to the National Portrait Gallery in London. The painter, George Richmond (1809–1896), also painted portraits of members of the English gentry, nobility, and royalty, as well as of other literary figures, including art critic John Ruskin and novelist George Eliot. Unlike Charlotte Brontë, George Eliot, author of *Middlemarch* and *The Mill on the Floss*, among other novels, continued to use her pen name throughout her career. Her name at birth was Mary Ann Evans.

promised to print. In the time it took him to publish the novels of Ellis and Acton Bell, however, *Jane Eyre* was published by a more honorable and scrupulous publisher, one who became a trusted friend. Newby, on the other hand, not only introduced many errors into Emily's text of *Wuthering Heights* and sowed confusion among the reading public as to the identity of the "Bells," but also never repaid any of the money advanced by Emily and Anne.

How did Charlotte's relationship with her publisher begin? In early August 1847, *The Professor* was rejected yet again. Unlike earlier rejection letters, however, this one held out the promise of hope. As Charlotte recalled in 1850, she opened that envelope "in the dreary expectation of finding two hard hopeless lines," but instead found a thoughtful two-page analysis of the "merits and demerits" of *The Professor*. The publisher's representative added that if she had another manuscript to submit, it "would meet with careful attention."[2]

A half century later, George Smith remembered the circumstances that led him to become both Charlotte's publisher and her friend: In July 1847, he had recently taken over the management of his father's publishing firm, Smith, Elder and Company, when "a parcel containing a MS. reached our office addressed to the firm, but bearing also the scored-out addresses of three or four other publishing houses; showing that the parcel had been previously submitted to other publishers. This was not calculated to prepossess us in favour of the MS. It was clear that we were offered what had been already rejected elsewhere." The manuscript of *The Professor* was read by Smith's literary assistant and publications manager, W. S. Williams. Williams reported to Smith that though *The Professor* "evinced great literary power," he doubted it would succeed in the marketplace. "We decided that he should write to 'Currer Bell' a letter of appreciative criticism declining the work, but expressing an opinion that he could produce a book which would command success." As it happened, Charlotte had just finished preparing the final manuscript of *Jane Eyre*, presenting it as "an autobiography, edited by Currer Bell." In short order, Charlotte sent it off to Smith, Elder. As Smith recalled, "The MS. of 'Jane Eyre' was read by Mr Williams in due course. He brought it to me on a Saturday, and said that he would like me to read it . . . . After breakfast on Sunday morning I took the MS. of 'Jane Eyre' to my little study, and began to read it. The story quickly took me captive." So caught up in the plot, Smith broke an appointment for that afternoon. He chose to eat a sandwich instead of his usual Sunday lunch, and when it was time for supper, "for me the meal was a very hasty one, and before I went to bed that night I had finished reading the manuscript. The next day we wrote to 'Currer Bell' accepting the book for publication."[3]

It took less than two months for Smith, Elder to publish their new find. So confident were they in the success of *Jane Eyre* that they sent a copy to William Makepeace Thackeray, an author they were courting. *Vanity Fair*, Thackeray's most famous novel, was in the process of being published in monthly installments when he received his copy of *Jane Eyre*. On October 23, 1847, four days after the publication of *Jane Eyre*, Thackeray sent W. S. Williams this unusual thank-you note: "I wish you had not sent me *Jane Eyre*. It interested me so much that I have lost (or won if you like) a whole day in reading it at the busiest period, with the printers I know waiting for copy . . . Give my respects and thanks to the author—whose novel is the first English one . . . that I've been able to read for many a day."[4]

Ever since 1847, readers have been just as reluctant as George Smith and William Makepeace Thackeray to put down their copy of *Jane Eyre* once they have begun to read it. Critics have also found countless ways to study and understand Charlotte Brontë's novel. Each year new books come out suggesting fresh approaches to the book, based on close readings. Careful reading of one's own may turn up aspects of *Jane Eyre* that Brontë scholars have not yet uncovered. While readers can be guided by previous critics' ideas, no reader should feel compelled to accept any one interpretation of the novel. The following section suggests one way to think about this novel of thirty-eight chapters, but encourages readers to find others on their own.

Encountering "Doubles" Along the Five Way Stations of a Spiritual Pilgrimage

In his initial response to "Currer Bell," W. S. Williams informed her that Smith, Elder would be glad to read carefully "a work in three volumes."[5] When the Brontës' novels appeared in the mid-nineteenth century, the principal format for publication of novels was the so-called three-decker, a work published in three separate volumes. Since books at the time were quite expensive, many readers borrowed them from lending libraries, rather than purchasing them themselves. Libraries normally restricted their patrons to one volume at a time, meaning that a single three-volume novel could serve three readers at once.

Today Charlotte's three main novels often appear without any indication that their contents were originally divided into three parts each. Despite the original three-volume format, however, the structure of *Jane Eyre* can be better thought of as a five-part one. Each part takes place in a different location. In each location, Jane encounters characters who are in some ways "doubles"—opposing or complementary versions of one another. Most often, the double serves to move the plot forward by presenting Jane with versions of herself that she must judge—and almost always surpass. Jane continually encounters, in the form of the double, options for herself that she must consider as she matures. Each of the book's locations marks a stage of Jane's spiritual pilgrimage. She learns in the course of the book to control her impulses. By doing so, she forges her own identity and establishes a personal relationship with God.

> **doubling**
>
> The depiction of pairs of characters to highlight similarities or differences between them.

Martha Abbot and Bessie, Mr. Lloyd and Mr. Brocklehurst: The Doubles at Gateshead

The novel opens in Gateshead Hall, the home of Jane's Uncle Reed, now dead. One critic has suggested that "the Reeds' home is the 'gate' at the 'head' of her journey through life."[6] On his deathbed, Uncle Reed extracted a promise from his wife, Aunt Sarah Reed, to care for their orphaned niece. Instead, Aunt Reed barely tolerates Jane and encourages her own children, Jane's cousins, to keep their distance from her. When her cousin John Reed interrupts while Jane is reading, he tells her, "You have no business to take our books; you are a dependent, mama says; you have no money; your father left you none; you ought to beg, and not to live here with gentlemen's children like us, and eat the same meals we do, and wear clothes at our mama's expense. Now, I'll teach you to rummage my bookshelves: for they are mine; all the house belongs to me, or will do in a few years."[7] He then strikes her with the book she had

This illustration from an early edition of *Jane Eyre* includes three characters: Mr. Brocklehurst—the supervisor of Lowood School to which Aunt Reed intends to send the unloved orphaned Jane; Aunt Reed; and Jane herself. The caption to the page is a quotation from Brocklehurst, speaking of the child: "Her size is small. What is her age?"

been reading, causing her to fall and cut her head. Rather than accepting his behavior passively, she lashes back at him with both words and fists. Jane's passionate reaction leads to a punishment.

On Mrs. Reed's instructions, two servants, Martha Abbot and Bessie, lock Jane up in solitary confinement in the "red room," where her Uncle Reed had died. As they overcome her resistance, Abbot tells her, "You are less than a servant, for you do nothing for your keep."[8] Abbot confirms her unsympathetic personality when she dismisses Jane by telling Bessie that "if she were a nice, pretty child, one might compassionate her forlornness; but one really cannot care for such a little toad as that."[9] Later on, Jane's self-description is hardly more favorable, as she calls herself "poor, obscure, plain and little."[10] Bessie, however, takes kind care of Jane when her extreme terror in the red room causes her to become so ill that Aunt Reed feels the need to call for the assistance of the apothecary, Mr. Lloyd.

Just as the two servants are doubles, Brontë presents a double for Mr. Lloyd. After hearing Jane's story for himself, Mr. Lloyd thinks correctly that she will not flourish in her aunt's home. On his advice, Aunt Reed decides to send Jane away to school. Jane is first interviewed by the school's director, Mr. Brocklehurst. He readily accepts Mrs. Reed's negative assessment of Jane and accuses her of having a "wicked heart."[11] Mr. Brocklehurst and Mr. Lloyd are contrasted both in the Gateshead section and in the Lowood School section that follows.

Miss Temple and Miss Scatcherd, Helen Burns and Jane: The Doubles at Lowood School

At Lowood, Jane finds two very different teachers: Miss Temple and Miss Scatcherd. Miss Scatcherd is quick to think the worst of the pupils, to beat them and subject them to public humiliation. Miss Temple, eager to think the best of everyone, tries to understand each girl's behavior. Through Miss Temple's actions with regard to Jane, the contrast between Mr. Brocklehurst and Mr. Lloyd continues to develop. Mr. Brocklehurst, son of the founder of the school and now its manager and treasurer, publicly announces that "the pious and charitable lady who adopted" Jane had been forced "to separate her from her own young ones, fearful lest her vicious example should contaminate their purity." Mr. Brocklehurst then warns her fellow pupils to shun Jane. He also warns Jane's teachers to keep a careful eye out for her and to "punish her body to save her soul."[12]

Miss Temple, however, is not willing to accept Mr. Brocklehurst's condemnation without exploring the charges more fully. She tells Jane, "when a criminal is accused, he is always allowed to speak in his own defence," and encourages Jane to have her say.[13] Jane's version of why she was expelled from Gateshead leads Miss Temple to write Mr. Lloyd for verification. Assured by Mr. Lloyd's response that Mr. Brocklehurst's accusations are baseless, Miss Temple clears Jane's reputation in front of the whole school. "The teachers then shook hands with me and kissed me, and a murmur of pleasure ran through the ranks of my companions."[14]

Another important female figure in Jane's Lowood years is the somewhat older pupil Helen Burns, who is a double for Jane herself. Well-read and able to speak several languages, Helen is an intellectual role model for Jane. On the other hand, Helen is also an example of what Jane must ultimately not be—self-denying to the point of death. As narrator of her own story, Jane describes in detail both Miss Scatcherd's beatings of Helen for sloppiness and Helen's tendency to turn the other cheek. Helen urges Jane to pay less attention to "the love of human beings" and more to the "invisible world," where "God waits only the separation of spirit from flesh to crown us with a full reward."[15] Helen eventually dies of tuberculosis in Jane's arms. Shortly before dying, she tells Jane, "I am going to God." Helen is secure in her faith, but Jane's series of questions reveal that the younger girl is not convinced. "Where is God? What is God?" she asks, and, "You are sure, then, Helen, that there is such a place as heaven; and that our souls can get to it when we die?" She also asks, "And shall I see you again, Helen, when I die?" Though Helen assures her that they will be reunited in "the same region of happiness," Jane remains doubtful, but she keeps her religious doubts to herself. "Again I questioned; but this time only in thought. 'Where is that region? Does it exist?'"[16]

Before the Lowood section of the novel closes, we learn of the school's transformation into "a truly useful and noble institution." Jane praises the "excellent education placed within my reach" and informs us that her success in her studies during her years there led her to be "invested with the office of teacher." From her association with Miss Temple, she has mastered the virtue of self-control so that "to the eyes of others, usually even to my own, I appeared a disciplined and subdued character." When Miss Temple leaves the school to get married, however, Jane discovers that without her calming influence, "I was left in my natural element, and beginning to feel the stirring of old emotions." She discovers that she is ready for something new: "now I remembered that the real world was wide, and that a varied field of hopes and fears, of sensations and excitements, awaited those who had courage to go forth into its expanse, to seek real knowledge of life amidst its perils."[17]

Bertha as Jane's Double at Thornfield

When Jane was sent off from Gateshead to Lowood, she understood she was embarking on a second stage in her life: "School would be a complete change: it implied a long journey, an entire separation from Gateshead, an entrance into a new life."[18] Now after eight years at Lowood, she knows it is again time for a new start. "I tired of the routine of eight years in one afternoon. I desired liberty; for liberty I gasped; for liberty I uttered a prayer."[19] With experience only as a teacher, a role she held for her final two years at Lowood, she advertises in a newspaper. Through this advertisement Jane secures a position at Thornfield, the home of her new employer, Edward Fairfax Rochester. There she becomes the governess of Adèle Varens, the daughter of one of Rochester's former mistresses. As Jane boards the "vehicle that was to bear me to new duties," she understands that in going off to her new position she is once again about to enter "a new life in . . . unknown environs."[20]

The "doubling" of characters that many critics note in the Thornfield section is more complicated than any of the others in the book. At Thornfield, Jane falls in love with Rochester and is on the verge of marrying him when she discovers he is already married. Years earlier, for financial reasons, Rochester's father had inveigled him into marrying Bertha Mason, the daughter of a wealthy Caribbean merchant. Soon after his marriage, Rochester discovered to his dismay that Bertha was, as he eventually tells Jane, "at once intemperate and unchaste."[21] Rochester has dealt with the situation by imprisoning the mentally unbalanced Bertha in Thornfield's attic, where she is under the care of a servant, Grace Poole. After his marriage to Jane is halted by these revelations, Rochester almost convinces Jane to live with him as a wife in every way except the exchanging of vows. The Thornfield section ends with Jane's decision not to yield to this temptation. Just as Jane had to reject modeling herself on her double Helen Burns, who represents all spirit at the expense of the physical body, she must also reject the path represented by Bertha—all body with no evident soul. Jane tells herself, "I will keep the law given by God; sanctioned by man. I will hold to the principles received by me when I was sane, and not mad—as I am now. Laws and principles are not for the times when there is no temptation . . . . They have a worth—so I have always believed; and if I cannot believe it now, it is because I am insane—quite insane."[22]

Based on Jane's own self-assessment that passion has made her insane and other hints in the novel, critics have pointed out the surprising ways in which Bertha is presented as Jane's double. One of the most memorable passages in *Jane Eyre* is Jane's passionate plea for women's rights that she expresses, if only to herself, shortly after her arrival at Thornfield, even before she meets Rochester.

> Women are supposed to be very calm generally: but women feel just as men feel; they need exercise for their faculties, and a field for their efforts as much as their brothers do; they suffer from too rigid a constraint, too absolute a stagnation, precisely as men would suffer; and it is narrow-minded in their more privileged fellow-creatures to say that they ought to confine themselves to making puddings and knitting stockings, to playing on the piano and embroidering bags. It is thoughtless to condemn them, or laugh at them, if they seek to do more or learn more than custom has pronounced necessary for their sex.[23]

Alert readers may note that shortly before that passage, Jane overhears "a curious laugh; distinct, formal mirthless." Though she is told by Mrs. Fairfax, the housekeeper, that the source of "that loud laugh" is "some of the servants, very likely, . . . perhaps Grace Poole," she later learns that "the laugh . . . as tragic, as preternatural a laugh as any I ever heard" emanated from Grace's patient, Bertha Mason Rochester.[24] Similarly, in the paragraph that immediately follows Jane's thoughts about women's need for employment and adventure, Jane tells us, "When thus alone, I not unfrequently heard Grace Poole's laugh; the same peal, the same low, slow ha! ha! which, when first heard, had thrilled me: I heard, too, her eccentric murmurs; stranger than her laugh."[25] According to poet Adrienne Rich, "Jane's sense of herself as a woman—as equal to and with the same needs as a man—is next-door to insanity in England in the 1840s . . . . there is a madwoman in the house who exists as her opposite . . . . Just as her instinct for self-preservation saves her from earlier temptations, so it must save her from becoming this woman."[26]

Critics have pointed to other hints in the novel that Bertha is Jane's double. For example, Jane's imprisonment in the red room at Gateshead for lashing out at her cousin John Reed has been compared to Bertha's imprisonment in the attic at Thornfield. Verbal echoes elsewhere also suggest a close relationship between Jane and Bertha. For example, Jane describes her restless nature, which leads her "to walk along the corridor of the third story, backwards and forwards."[27] When Rochester finally takes Jane to the room where Bertha is confined, she sees "a figure [that] ran backwards and forwards. What it was, whether beast or human being, one could not, at first sight, tell."[28]

This handwritten first page of *Jane Eyre* is held by the British Library. The library's description of this item notes not only the pen name "Currer Bell" at the top of the page, but also the neatness of Charlotte's handwriting.

The identification of Bertha as "the madwoman in the attic" was made famous by critics Sandra Gilbert and Susan Gubar in a 1979 book by that title.[29] Their book, which became a classic of feminist literary criticism, examined the idea that nineteenth-century female writers were shaped by the personal and professional restrictions that society imposed on women at that time. According to Gilbert and Gubar, Bertha is in a sense the double not only of Jane but also of Charlotte Brontë, whose own anger at society the fictional character represents.

The doubling of the English heroine Jane and the West Indian Bertha Rochester has inspired not only feminist criticism but also what is called postcolonial criticism. At the time Charlotte Brontë was writing, the British rationalized the colonization of far-flung territories as their mission to bring civilization to savages. While Rochester describes himself as an innocent victim of the lascivious West Indian Bertha, postcolonial critics point to him instead as a victimizer who set out for the West Indies to enrich himself at the expense of the native population. In the view of postcolonial critics, Charlotte Brontë, the product of her times, accepted the stereotypes of English purity and cultural superiority that prevailed in her day.

St. John Rivers as Rochester's Double at Marsh End

Before Jane reaches Marsh End (also called Moor House), the location where the fourth section of the book takes place, she nearly dies of starvation and exposure. She is taken in by the Rivers family—two sisters, Diana and Mary, and their brother, St. John (pronounced "Sinjin")—who turn out to be Jane's cousins. As such, these compassionate, like-minded relatives are also doubles for Jane's Reed cousins, with whom she has nothing but blood in common. At Marsh End, St. John Rivers, a clergyman determined to go to India as a missionary, proposes marriage to Jane. She inevitably compares her feelings toward St. John with her feelings toward Rochester. These feelings have nothing to do with looks. In Jane's eyes, Rochester's features are "not beautiful, according to rule," but rather "full of an interest, an influence that quite mastered me." Nonetheless, she falls in love with Rochester because she feels that despite their differences in "rank and wealth," "something in my brain and heart, in my blood and nerves . . . assimilates me mentally to him."[30] By contrast, Jane finds that St. John's face "riveted the eye; it was like a Greek face,"[31] but she feels only admiration, not love, for him, and understands that he feels no love for her. She asks herself, "Can I receive from him the bridal ring, endure all the forms of love . . . and know that the spirit was quite absent?"[32] Jane suggests that she accompany St. John to India but only as a sister, not a wife. Rejecting Jane's suggestion, St. John tries to convince her that "undoubtedly enough of love would follow upon marriage to render the union right even in your eyes." When she retorts, "I scorn your idea of love," he accuses her of denying God's will by rejecting his proposal.[33]

St. John makes a final attempt to persuade Jane, but she holds her ground: "God did not give me my life to throw away; and to do as you wish me would, I begin to think, be almost equivalent to committing suicide."[34] Even so, Jane nearly yields to St. John's request. She tells him that "were I but convinced that it is God's will I should marry, you, I could vow to marry you here and now."[35] Even as St. John thanks God for hearing his prayers, Jane hears something else: "the voice of a human being—a known, loved, well-remembered voice—that of Edward Fairfax Rochester," calling out her name.[36] Convinced that this voice is really a call from God, she goes to her room, where she prays in her own way to God. "I seemed to penetrate very near a Mighty Spirit; and my soul rushed out in gratitude at His feet."[37] Jane responds to what she perceives as God's call by rushing off to see Rochester.

An Unexpected Ending at Ferndean

The final section of *Jane Eyre* consists of only three chapters, taking Jane from her rejection of marriage at Marsh End to marriage with Rochester at Ferndean, his second and much less grand house. Finding Thornfield burned to the ground, Jane learns that Bertha set the house on fire before hurling herself off the roof to her death. Determined to make sure that all the occupants of the house were evacuated before he himself left for safety, Rochester was blinded when the staircase crumbled under him. The accident also crushed one of his hands so badly that it had to be amputated.

During their reunion, Jane learns that the experience has made Rochester a more spiritual man: "Of late, Jane . . . I began to see and acknowledge the hand of God in my doom."[38] He tells her that a few nights before, yearning for her, "with soul and flesh," he "asked of God . . . if I had not been long enough desolate, afflicted, tormented; and might not soon taste bliss and peace once more." As he did so, "the alpha and omega of my heart's wishes broke involuntarily from my lips in the words—'Jane! Jane! Jane!'"[39] "Alpha and omega" are not only the first and last letters of the ancient Greek alphabet but also are used together as a name for God in the New Testament Book of Revelation. The next-to-last chapter in *Jane Eyre*, chapter 37, then ends with the image of Jane and Rochester walking hand in hand back to Ferndean. (Remembering that the Brontë children had been introduced to the works of

HEARING VOICES FROM AFAR IN *JANE EYRE*: A CLUE FROM BRUSSELS

In her 2015 biography, *Charlotte Brontë: A Fiery Heart*, author Claire Harman sheds interesting light on the scenes in *Jane Eyre* when Jane hears Rochester's voice from afar and when she later learns from Rochester himself that he did, in fact, longingly call out her name. According to Gaskell, as Harman notes, Charlotte once defended to a challenger the possibility of communicating in this fashion, saying, "But it is a true thing; it really happened." Gaskell assumed that Charlotte was talking about her own experience of communicating with her deceased two older siblings, for whom she still grieved. Harman, however, has epistolary evidence from Brussels that suggests otherwise. In the late 1880s—four decades following the publication of *Jane Eyre*—Monsieur Heger, Charlotte's teacher with whom she had become infatuated, wrote another favorite student from England about the possibility of communicating through emotional telepathy. Charlotte would have been elated had her professor written her as he wrote Meta Mossman that "I have only to think of you to see you...I see you, I talk with you...just as I knew you, my dear."[40] Harman wonders whether Heger had ever described this kind of communication with Charlotte while she was still his student: "Was it his habit to attempt such mental communion across long distances and adverse circumstances?" In the final sentence of this interesting biography, however, Harman turns that question on its head. "Or had he simply been reading *Jane Eyre*?"[41] In other words, did life—a conversation with Heger— influence Charlotte Brontë's fiction, or did Charlotte Brontë's fiction influence life—Heger's letter to a former student?

Jane and Rochester in a scene from the 2011 film version of *Jane Eyre*, starring Mia Wasikowska as Jane and Michael Fassbender as Rochester. In a four-word summary of his reaction to the film, *New York Times* reviewer A. O. Scott riffs on the novel's famous line "Reader, I married him," by writing, "Reader, I liked it."

John Milton as children, we can detect the influence on this concluding image of the last lines of Book XII of Milton's *Paradise Lost*, in which the poet describes Adam and Eve on their expulsion from the Garden of Eden in these terms:

> "They, hand in hand, with wandering steps and slow,
> Through Eden took their solitary way."

If Jane's spiritual pilgrimage ends in marriage at Ferndean, the novel concludes almost but not quite with the expected fairy-tale ending: Jane and Rochester enjoy a marriage of equals, never running out of things to discuss, and Rochester regains enough of his sight to be able to see that "his first-born . . . boy had inherited his own eyes, as they once were—large, brilliant, and black."[42] But the chapter that begins with Jane's famous statement, "Reader, I married him," ends with three paragraphs devoted neither to Jane nor to Rochester, but rather to St. John Rivers, and the last lines of the novel are a quotation from the book of Revelation. Perhaps Brontë, the daughter of a clergyman and for years a devoted Sunday-school teacher, wants us to appreciate that marriage—even of the happiest kind—is not the only way to fulfill one's purpose in life. While Jane's rejection of St. John Rivers's proposal was the right choice for her, she recognizes the spiritual value of the choice St. John has made for himself.

An Oblivious Father's Reaction to a Daughter's Novel

We do not know how the Reverend Brontë interpreted the conclusion of Charlotte's novel. We do know, however, a story about his overall response to it. According to Elizabeth Gaskell, at her sisters' insistence, Charlotte brought a copy of the published novel to her father in his study and told him she had written a book she would like him to read. He begged off, concerned that reading a manuscript would "try my eyes too much." When she told him that the book had been printed and published, he chastised her: "My dear! you've never thought of the expense it will be! It will be almost sure to be a loss; for how can you get a book sold? No one knows you or your name." Before giving him the book, she responded, "But, papa, I don't think it will be a loss; no more will you, if you will just let me read you a review or two, and tell you more about it." Once she had done so, Charlotte gave him the novel to read. "When he came in to tea he said, 'Girls, do you know Charlotte has been writing a book, and it is much better than likely?'"[43]

It is unlikely that the Reverend Brontë would have commented so favorably on his daughter Emily's book, which came out two months after the publication of *Jane Eyre*.

A One-of-a-Kind Novel: Ellis Bell's *Wuthering Heights*

Charlotte was better served by her choice of publisher than Emily and Anne were in theirs. Thomas Newby not only waited to publish the novels by Currer Bell's "brothers" until several months after Currer's work had proven a smash hit, but he also intentionally publicized Ellis's novel as "by the author of *Jane Eyre.*" This confusion of identity was an affront not only to the actual author of *Wuthering Heights* but also to the author of *Jane Eyre.*

The main narrator of *Wuthering Heights*, Mr. Lockwood, explains the meaning of the title in his characteristically pompous way: It is "a significant provincial adjective, descriptive of the atmospheric tumult."[1] In other words, "wuthering" refers to stormy weather. In her 1850 "Editor's Preface to the New Edition of *Wuthering Heights*," Charlotte suggests that the atmosphere in the sisters' writing workshop might have been just as stormy when Emily read aloud from her novel in progress. According to Charlotte: "If the auditor of her work when read in manuscript, shuddered under the grinding influence of natures so relentless and implacable, of spirits so lost and fallen; if it was complained that the mere hearing of certain vivid and fearful scenes banished sleep by night, and disturbed mental peace by day, Ellis Bell would wonder what was meant, and suspect the complainant of affectation."[2]

This portrait of Emily at the age of approximately fifteen was drawn by Branwell as part of the original "Gun Group" painting, shown in chapter 3. The only part of that work to survive, the portrait was restored in 1999 by artist Michael Armitage.

While Charlotte and Anne clearly objected to scenes in Emily's novel, it seems likely that Emily simply did not care what other people thought. In her poem "To Imagination," Emily wrote proudly: "I have persevered to shun/The common paths that others run."[3] According to Elizabeth Gaskell, "Emily was impervious to influence; she never came in contact with public opinion, and her own decision of what was right and fitting was a law for her conduct and appearance, with which she allowed no one to interfere."[4] She would probably have taken pleasure in reviews that deplored the violence in the book but also spoke of its power. One reviewer, for example, wrote: "In spite of the disgusting coarseness of much of the dialogue, and the improbabilities and incongruities of the plot, we are spell-bound, we cannot choose but read."[5] Another said, "There seems to us great power in this book but a purposeless power, which we feel a great desire to see turned to better account."[6]

Possible Influences on the Development of *Wuthering Heights*

Unlike the case with *Jane Eyre*, we do not know when Emily began *Wuthering Heights*. No manuscript survives to indicate how she developed the novel. One of Emily's recent biographers, Edward Chitham, suggests that she may have begun a version of the novel as early as 1839. The fact that Emily wrote no poetry then, during her second term as a teacher at Law Hill School, might indicate that she was working on an early draft of what became *Wuthering Heights*. Whether or not she did so, Chitham notes that the history of the school may have influenced the development of the character of Heathcliff. On one level, the complicated story of *Wuthering Heights* is the tale of a usurper—someone who takes possession of something through force. Heathcliff, an outsider brought into the Earnshaw family, takes revenge on the Earnshaw and Linton families for mistreating him by taking over their possessions. While at Law Hill, Emily might well have learned about a local wool merchant whose adopted nephew encouraged the merchant's true heir to gamble excessively and degraded a young cousin of the heir. In *Wuthering Heights,* Heathcliff similarly encourages Hindley Earnshaw to go into debt through gambling and takes revenge on Hindley's having degraded him by degrading Hindley's son.

According to Chitham, from childhood Emily would have heard her father tell stories of two other usurpers. Patrick Brontë's father, Hugh Brunty, claimed to have been deprived of his birthright by his wicked Uncle Welsh, an orphan who had been discovered on a Liverpool boat. Charlotte's friend Ellen Nussey claimed that the roots of Emily's novel lay in the frightening stories, which made one "shiver and shrink from hearing," which the Reverend Brontë would tell about "the extraordinary lives and doings of people who resided . . . in contiguity with Haworth."[7]

Another story of a usurper lay closer to home than Ireland. Ponden Hall, home of the Heaton family, about 2 miles (3.2 km) from the parsonage, was a place at which the Brontës often stopped during their walks. For a period of twenty years in the seventeenth century, the husband of a Heaton widow took illegal control of the family holdings. After the usurper's death, the true heir, Robert Heaton, had to buy back what was rightfully his. The first chapter of *Wuthering Heights* begins not with a word but with a date: "1801." That same date appeared over the lintel—a horizontal support of timber, stone, concrete, or steel across the top of a door or window—of Ponden Hall, indicating the year the house was rebuilt. Chitham also suggests that the name "Hareton" is an anagram (a word or name made by rearranging the letters of another word or name) of the name R. Heaton. In *Wuthering Heights*, Hareton Earnshaw is the name of the rightful heir to Wuthering Heights, the property of the Earnshaw family, whose inheritance Heathcliff usurps. It is also the name of his ancestor whose name is carved over the door of Wuthering Heights.

Chitham believes that Emily must have had to double the length of *Wuthering Heights* in August 1846. At that time, the publisher Thomas Newby declined to publish Charlotte's *The Professor*, which had been submitted to him along with Anne's *Agnes Grey* and Emily's *Wuthering Heights*

> **anagram**
>
> A word or name made by rearranging the letters of another word or name.

as one of three volumes. (Remember that Charlotte sent off the three sisters' novels as "a work of fiction—consisting of three distinct and unconnected tales,"[8] so that they could be printed as a three-decker.) When Newby published the other two novels in 1847, Emily's filled two volumes and Anne's only one. As Chitham says, "It hardly seems possible that the same version of *Wuthering Heights* should be worth one volume in 1846 and two in 1847."[9] One possibility is that the original volume told the story only of Catherine Earnshaw and Heathcliff. According to Chitham, "Emily Brontë's . . . exploration of the life of a second Catherine was only made possible by a change of plan forced on her and Anne after the original version had been submitted and rejected."[10] Chitham suggests that Newby may have accepted *Wuthering Heights* for publication only on the condition that Emily both increase its length and soften its tone. Adding the story of the second generation

In 1964, the Brontë Society affixed a plaque at Top Withens, the abandoned farmhouse shown here, reading, "This farmhouse has been associated with *Wuthering Heights*, the Earnshaw home in Emily Brontë's novel. The buildings, even when complete, bore no resemblance to the house she described, but the situation may have been in her mind when she wrote of the moorland setting of the Heights."

would have enabled her to do both. Catherine Linton is able to reverse Heathcliff's debasement of Hareton by educating him. Through their marriage, the Earnshaw fortune is restored to its rightful heir. Their union also resolves the class conflict between the Lintons—representatives of the gentry, who hired laborers to cultivate their land—and the Earnshaws—representatives of the yeomanry, who farmed their own land.

Wuthering Heights: A Novel with Several Narrators

Literary critics exploring Emily Brontë's novel from many angles agree that while "*Wuthering Heights* is a striking achievement of some kind . . . there is no agreed reading of this novel at all."[11] There is no point in trying to analyze this or any other novel in the hopes that if we search hard enough we can find in it "a code, or a nut, that can be broken; which contains or refers to a meaning all will agree upon if it can once be presented *en clair*."[12] The very fact that the novel is considered a classic means that it can be interpreted in many different ways.

> In her 1850 editor's preface to the second edition, Charlotte suggests that the writer who possesses the creative gift owns something of which he is not always master—something that at times strangely wills and works for itself . . . . Be the work grim or glorious, dread or divine, you have little choice left but quiescent adoption. As for you—the nominal artist—your share in it has been to work passively under dictates you neither delivered nor could question . . . . If the result be attractive, the World will praise you, who little deserve praise; if it be repulsive, the same World will blame you, who almost as little deserve blame.[13]

Charlotte wrote these words in order to defend Emily against reviewers who were put off by the brutality and darkness of much of *Wuthering Heights*, whose scenes of savage cruelty include the dream image of a child's wrist being dragged across broken glass until the sheets are soaked in her blood.[14] Charlotte's suggestion, however, that Emily was not master of her own novel is clearly incorrect. Scholars have noted how carefully she worked out chronologies and family histories, how detailed her knowledge of English laws of inheritance was, and how meticulously she would check almanacs to correlate weather and lunar phenomena with dates. One feature of the novel that shows how carefully she worked, and how intentionally she left the meaning of her novel unclear, is the attention she paid to the narrative structure of the book.

The narrative structure of *Wuthering Heights* has been compared to a Chinese box—a matched set of boxes of decreasing size, so that each one fits snugly inside the next. The image is appropriate because the book has several different narrators. The main narrator is Lockwood, the keeper of the diary in which the pompous explanation of the novel's title is given. Lockwood's diary also includes the narration of Ellen, or Nelly, Dean, the unmarried housekeeper of Thrushcross Grange. Nelly grew up at Wuthering Heights and also served there. Nestled inside Nelly's narrative are not only eyewitness reports but also a letter from Heathcliff's abused wife, Isabella Linton, and accounts from Zillah, who serves as housekeeper at Wuthering Heights while Heathcliff controls it. When Heathcliff bans Nelly from the Heights, Zillah serves as Nelly's informant as to what goes on there.

The book is presented as two sets of entries in Lockwood's diary, which together tell the story of the Earnshaw and Linton families. The first set of entries date from 1801, when Lockwood, after an unsuccessful attempt at romance in a seaside resort in the south of England, decides to retreat from society by renting Thrushcross Grange from Heathcliff, its current owner. Although the Grange was originally the property of the Linton family, Heathcliff has taken it over as part of his plan to exact revenge. Lockwood becomes ill when he decides during a snowstorm to drop in on Heathcliff at Wuthering Heights. As part of his revenge, Heathcliff has also taken over Wuthering Heights, originally the property of the Earnshaws. While Lockwood recovers from his illness, Nelly tells him the story of the inhabitants of both houses over the past thirty years: the complicated interactions among Heathcliff; his wife, Isabella; her estranged brother, Edgar Linton; and Catherine Earnshaw Linton, who, even though she knew Heathcliff was her soulmate, had married Edgar.

Lockwood's second set of entries begins in September 1802, when on his way north for the shooting season, he pays a call on Nelly. This visit allows her to tell him the story of Heathcliff's death and the engagement of Hareton Earnshaw and Catherine Linton. As one critic has remarked, "during a major part of the book Mr Lockwood is telling us what Ellen Dean told him, but sometimes, also, what Ellen Dean told him that someone else—for instance, Isabella—had told her. Only a small part, perhaps one-tenth of the book, consists of direct narrative by Lockwood from his own knowledge."[15]

Neither Lockwood nor Nelly is a reliable narrator. From the very beginning, it is clear Lockwood lacks understanding of his own motives and actions, much less those of the strange people he encounters at Wuthering Heights. No matter how upsetting what he learns from Nelly is, he is determined to put a positive spin on it. When other duties lead Nelly to interrupt her tale, she tells Lockwood, "My history is dree as we say."

He records in his diary, using the same Yorkshire dialect word for "sad": "Dree, and dreary! . . . But never mind! I'll extract wholesome medicines from Mrs. Dean's bitter herbs."[16]

If Lockwood is too naïvely upbeat to be a reliable narrator of the strange interlocking stories of the inhabitants of Wuthering Heights and Thrushcross Grange, Nelly Dean is too involved to be reliable. She often plays a role in the events she is relating and so is hardly objective. For example, by letting Heathcliff visit the pregnant and ill Catherine during her husband's absence, Nelly is complicit in bringing about the premature childbirth that leads to Catherine's death. She is also too conventional a person, too grounded in social pieties, to know what to make of the intense emotions she witnesses. In one of the most passionate speeches in English literature, Catherine confides in Nelly her decision to marry Edgar, despite the fact that Heathcliff is "more myself than I am."[17] Nelly's response to Catherine's unburdening of her soul is that "you are ignorant of the duties you undertake in marrying; or else . . . you are a wicked, unprincipled girl."[18] When Catherine dies, Nelly ignores Catherine's earlier remark that "if I were in heaven, Nelly, I should be extremely miserable."[19] She tells Heathcliff that her mistress is "gone to heaven, I hope, where we may, everyone, join her, if we take due warning, and leave our evil ways to follow good."[20]

Emily Brontë's complex narrative strategy—"the absence of any trustworthy and knowing narrator who clearly speaks for the author"—is one of the ways she keeps the reader off balance.[21] The implication is that the story Lockwood and Nelly try to tell is too powerful to be contained within the normal bounds of fiction.

Wuthering Heights and Thrushcross Grange: Comparing Two Houses

Many readers interpret *Wuthering Heights* as Emily Brontë's exploration of the theme of good versus evil. In doing so, according to this reading, Brontë uses the homes of the main characters symbolically, with Thrushcross Grange representing Good (including such attributes as heaven, light, and peace) and Wuthering Heights representing Evil (with the opposing attributes of hell, darkness, and rivalry). Wuthering Heights is described in threatening terms, adorned as it is with "a quantity of grotesque carving" and fitted with "narrow windows deeply set in the wall," whose "corners defended with large jutting stones"[22] suggest the paranoid fears of its inhabitants. The house also conveys a "pervading spirit of neglect;"[23] neither plants nor other living things, including human beings, can grow normally there.

By contrast, when young Cathy and Heathcliff, early in the novel, peer into the interior of Thrushcross Grange, they are overwhelmed by its elegance and tranquility: "Both of us were able to look in by standing on the basement, and clinging to the ledge, and we saw—ah! it was beautiful—a splendid place carpeted with crimson, and crimson-covered chairs and tables, and a pure white ceiling bordered by gold, a shower of glass-drops hanging in silver chains from the centre, and shimmering with little soft tapers." Nonetheless, the voyeurs can see that its inhabitants are not happy. Heathcliff glimpses Isabella "screaming at the farther end of the room, shrieking as if witches were running red-hot needles into her," while Edgar "stood on the hearth weeping silently."[24] Even the dog seems out of sorts.

Thrushcross Grange may be the place to which Catherine is taken when she falls ill at Wuthering Heights, but Catherine stunts her own growth when she chooses the refinement of the Grange over the passion she feels for Heathcliff and Wuthering Heights. The light-skinned, light-haired, superficially well-mannered inhabitants of the Grange are less resilient than Heathcliff, who embodies the spirit and passion of Wuthering Heights. Although the novel concludes with the impending marriage of Catherine Linton and Hareton Earnshaw, and a seeming triumph of civilization over unrestrained passion, Emily Brontë is too determined to keep the reader off-balance to let the contrast between good and evil be too pat. If the unreliable narrator Lockwood can imagine at the end that Catherine, Edgar, and Heathcliff will all rest in peace in their graves, readers can feel free to doubt just how sunny the ending truly is, with its fixation on decaying corpses.

Heathcliff's Uncertain Identity

Another feature of the novel that shows Emily Brontë's determination to leave questions unanswered is her treatment of Heathcliff. Many questions about Heathcliff's origins remain unanswered. In chapter 4, we learn that old Mr. Earnshaw returns home from a trip to Liverpool with a waif he found on the streets "starving, and houseless, and as good as dumb."[25] This foundling is soon christened with "the name of a son who died in childhood."[26] Earnshaw favors Heathcliff over his own children and is particularly upset to discover his son Hindley persecuting the "poor fatherless child."[27] Some readers conclude that Heathcliff must be Mr. Earnshaw's illegitimate son. If so, Catherine and he would be half siblings, and their love for one another would be scandalous from the outset.

Critics in recent years have studied the history of Liverpool at the time Mr. Earnshaw would have made his trip there. What they have uncovered has only deepened the mystery about Heathcliff's origins. Liverpool was both the center for Irish immigration into England and a major port for the importation of African slaves. In August 1845, Branwell Brontë came back from Liverpool with stories of the starving children among the shiploads of Irish immigrants coming into the port. Nelly's description of Heathcliff as "a dirty, ragged, black-

WUTHERING HEIGHTS

Heathcliff (LAURENCE OLIVIER) carries Cathy (MERLE OBERON), who has become weak from illness, to see the fields of heather in WUTHERING HEIGHTS, a Samuel Goldwyn Company presentation.

THE SAMUEL GOLDWYN COMPANY

© 1989 THE SAMUEL GOLDWYN COMPAN

A scene from the 1939 film version of *Wuthering Heights*, starring Laurence Olivier as Heathcliff and Merle Oberon as Catherine. In 2007, this film directed by William Wyler was designated for preservation in the Library of Congress's National Film Registry.

haired child"[28] suggests that he might have been a forerunner of one of the hungry Irish newcomers Branwell encountered in Liverpool. On the other hand, Mr. Earnshaw describes the child Heathcliff as "dark almost as if it came from the devil," speaking "some gibberish that nobody could understand,"[29] which suggests he might have arrived in Liverpool among the black slaves who were put to work in Yorkshire farms in the eighteenth century. The elder Lintons later describe Heathcliff as "a gypsy" and as "a little Lascar, or an American or Spanish castaway."[30] While "Lascar" is a term for an Asian seaman, "American" or "Spanish" might refer to a slave from the North or South American colonies.

Another mystery that Emily Brontë leaves unsolved is what Heathcliff does during a crucial three-year period. In chapter 8, Heathcliff overhears Catherine say that marrying him would degrade her. He then disappears for three years, after which he returns as a dignified and well-to-do man with a foreign accent. Lockwood offers some suggestions to account for Heathcliff's miraculous transformation: Perhaps he got an education either abroad or in England, or served as a soldier in America, or made a fortune either legitimately or as a highwayman. The facts are withheld, and we never know the answer to Nelly's question: "Is he a ghoul, or a vampire? . . . where did he come from, the little dark thing, harboured by a good man to his bane?"[31]

We sympathize with Heathcliff when Hindley mistreats him, but his gratuitous violence to Isabella and his ruthless revenge on Hindley and the Lintons make us ask, along with Isabella, "Is he a devil?"[32] Yet there is no dismissing his obsessive passion for Catherine, which leads to some of the most powerful expressions of love in all of literature. Even his mad but ultimately successful scheme to mingle his remains with hers in the grave arouses something like admiration in the reader. We are left with mixed feelings about Heathcliff, as we are about each character in this one-of-a-kind novel. The novel closes with two alternative resolutions: Do the ghosts of Heathcliff and Catherine walk at night, encountering the locals, as Nelly reports? Or is Lockwood right when he looks at the grave that encloses the remains of Edgar, Catherine, and Heathcliff and wonders "how any one could ever imagine unquiet slumbers for the sleepers in that quiet earth."[33]

This fifteen-pence English postage stamp celebrating Emily Brontë and *Wuthering Heights* is part of the 1980 commemorative series recognizing "Famous Authoresses." The other three women to be thus honored include Charlotte Brontë (for *Jane Eyre*), Elizabeth Gaskell (for *North and South*), and George Eliot (for *The Mill on the Floss*).

WHAT BECAME OF EMILY BRONTË'S PERSONAL COPY OF HER PUBLISHED NOVEL?

For over a century, it was believed that Emily's copy of the published *Wuthering Heights*, containing her handwritten corrections, was in the collection of Charlotte's widower, Arthur Bell Nicholls. When the book was sold in 1969, however, it turned out that the handwriting was Charlotte's. Like so much else about Emily Brontë, we are unlikely ever to know what became of her own copy of her novel.

Heathcliff has roots not only in real-life stories but also in Emily's Gondal writing. Her hero Julius Brenzaida, for example, was a usurper who succeeded in becoming emperor of Gondal. And according to Emily's biographer Edward Chitham, "Emily herself has aspects of Heathcliff in her."[34] In the novel, Heathcliff hangs his wife Isabella's pet dog. In Elizabeth Gaskell's biography of Charlotte, we learn that Emily once brutally beat her own beloved dog, Keeper, for lying on the white quilts that covered the parsonage beds: "her bare clenched fist struck against his fierce eyes, before he had time to make his spring . . . she 'punished him' till his eyes were swelled up, and the half-blind stupefied beast was led to his accustomed lair, to have his swelled head . . . cared for by the very Emily herself."[35] If Gaskell's story leaves us uncertain how to respond to Emily's excessive behavior, Emily's depiction of Heathcliff makes it difficult for readers to know whether to sympathize with or deplore his actions.

Did Emily Have Another Novel in Her?

Although *Wuthering Heights* is the only novel by Emily Brontë ever to be published, in Charlotte's "Biographical Notice," written after the deaths of her sisters, she implied that both of her sisters had other novels in them and perhaps had begun to work on them: "They were both prepared to try again."[36] There is evidence that Emily probably was at work on a second novel during the last year of her life. The Brontë sisters had portable writing boxes that they carried around with them to use as desks. Sometime after Emily's death on December 19, 1848, her "desk-box" was opened. It contained five reviews of *Wuthering Heights* and a letter from her publisher, Thomas Newby. Although the letter is addressed only to "Dear Sir," its envelope bears the name "Ellis Bell, Esq." There is no address on the letter, but it is possible that Newby sent the letter in an enclosure to a letter addressed to "Acton Bell, Esq."—namely, Anne.

The text of the note from Newby indicates that it is a response to a previous note from Emily: "I am much obliged by your kind note & shall have great pleasure in making arrangements for your next novel I would not hurry its completion, for I think you are quite right not to let it go before the world until well satisfied with it, for much depends on your next work if it be an improvement on your first you will have established yourself as a first rate novelist, but if it fall short the Critics will be too apt to say that you have expended your talent in your first novel."[37]

What was Emily Brontë's new novel about? What became of it? Did Charlotte destroy it, either of her own accord or on Emily's deathbed instructions? We are unlikely ever to know. Emily Brontë went to her death leaving unsolved mysteries not only about her only published novel but also about the contents of what would have been, had she lived, her second novel.

Last but Not Least: Acton Bell's Two Novels

Imagine that you are being remembered two hundred years after your birth. Although you have left behind a significant body of work—two novels, some poems, some drawings, a piece of sewing—archivists have been able to find only five letters you wrote in your lifetime and a couple of "diary papers" that summarize some reflections on your life at the moment. Biographers are interested in writing about you, but they find themselves having to rely on discussions of you in other people's letters and diaries. They also probe your novels and poems for information about you. How accurate a picture of you do you think they will be able to put together in this manner? This situation describes scholarly attempts to portray the life of Anne Brontë, the youngest of the Brontë siblings.

Anne Brontë was certainly neither the first nor the last youngest child who had to struggle to be taken seriously by her older siblings. Charlotte's attitude toward Anne was protective but also dismissive. In 1834, by which time Anne was a young teenager, Charlotte wrote a medley of scenes including descriptions of some of her favorite Angrian characters. One character is a caricature of Branwell, whom she calls Patrick Benjamin Wiggins. Charlotte attributes to Wiggins the following assessment of his youngest sister: "Anne is nothing, absolutely nothing," a sentiment with which

This portrait of Anne Brontë was painted in watercolors by
Charlotte, who signed and dated it "June 17, 1834," when her
subject was fourteen years old.

Charlotte apparently agreed.[1] In an 1839 letter to her school friend Ellen Nussey, Charlotte wrote with surprise about the maturity of Anne's first letter from her job as a governess: "You would be astonished what a sensible, clever letter she writes."[2] Eleven years later, in her "Biographical Notice" of her sisters, Charlotte compared Anne unfavorably to Emily: "She wanted the power, the fire, the originality of her sister, but was well endowed with quiet virtues of her own."[3] Years after all the sisters had died, Charlotte's opinion of Anne still carried weight with Ellen, who condescendingly wrote in 1871, "Anne, dear gentle Anne."[4]

This kind of dismissive reference to Anne soon spread beyond family and friends. In 1897, one critic asserted that Anne's claim to fame was entirely "due to her sisters." Another wrote, echoing Ellen Nussey, "The youngest of all, the gentle Anne, would have no right to be considered at all as a writer but for her association" with her much more accomplished sisters.[5]

Recently, however, Brontë scholars have reconsidered Anne's work and reputation. Far from being "nothing" or passively "gentle," Anne was the author of two novels, both of which argue on behalf of equal treatment of the sexes in education, professional opportunities, and marriage. Anne's second novel, *The Tenant of Wildfell Hall*, sold nearly as well as Charlotte's best-selling *Jane Eyre*. Anne's first novel, *Agnes Grey*, was often dismissed as a pale imitation of *Jane Eyre*, which was published a few months before it. Since *Agnes Grey* was written considerably before *Jane Eyre*, however, and Charlotte knew it well from the sisters' workshop sessions, Charlotte was able to model her heroine and novel on patterns Anne was the first to devise. New research has also demonstrated that, through her novels, Anne criticized what she saw as serious deficiencies in both Charlotte's and Emily's work.

Anne's literary goals differed from those of her sisters. Emily and Charlotte adapted the flamboyant and risqué style and content of their juvenilia to craft their famous works, each in her own way. Anne was much more of a moralist than either of her sisters. She believed that fiction should be morally instructive. Fiction should not shirk from the seamy realities of life, but it should not make them attractive. Instead, fiction should help people live more ethical and meaningful lives.

Anne was also the most deeply religious of the sisters. As daughters of a clergyman, all three knew the Bible inside and out. Emily was the least conventionally religious of the three and the only one not to teach Sunday school. In *Wuthering Heights*, through the character of the servant Joseph, she takes potshots at those who "ever ransacked a Bible to rake the promises to himself and fling the curses on his neighbours."[6] Although Charlotte clearly demonstrated the faults of Mr. Brocklehurst in *Jane Eyre* and poked fun at a variety of churchmen in her next novel, *Shirley*, religion was important to her, and Jane's story is one of a spiritual pilgrimage. For Anne, however, the conviction that she must do good and teach God's message was the central motivating factor of her life. Having experienced a religious crisis while a student at Miss Wooler's school, she wrote *Agnes Grey* and *The Tenant of Wildfell Hall* with the intention of strengthening her readers' faith and helping them avoid sin. As the heroine of *Agnes Grey* says, "The end of Religion is not to teach us how to die, but how to live; and the earlier you become wise and good, the more of happiness you secure."[7]

Comparing Two Novels About Governesses

Agnes Grey is the story of a young woman, not yet twenty at the outset, who makes her own way in the world as a governess. It draws on Anne's own experiences as a governess in two different households. Anne's novel was already making the rounds of publishers before Charlotte began writing *Jane Eyre* in the summer of 1846.

In her *Life of Charlotte Brontë*, Elizabeth Gaskell passes on a story that Charlotte supposedly told about the origin of her governess heroine. After Charlotte's death, Harriet Martineau, another woman writer who was for a time Charlotte's friend, wrote in an obituary, "She once told her sisters they were wrong—even morally wrong—in making their heroines beautiful, as a matter of course. They replied that it was impossible to make a heroine interesting on other terms. Her answer was, 'I will prove to you that you are wrong. I will show you a heroine as small and plain as myself who shall be as interesting as any of yours.'"[8] If Martineau's recollection was correct, Charlotte was stretching the truth. Her youngest sister had already created in Agnes Grey a heroine of ordinary looks. Charlotte had certainly heard Anne read her novel in progress at their workshop sessions. She seems to have been inspired in several ways by what she heard. She not only made the heroine of her second novel an ordinary-looking governess but also made her the narrator, as Agnes is in Anne's novel. *Jane Eyre* marks Charlotte's first use of a female narrator. Her first novel, *The Professor*, is narrated by a man, William Crimsworth. In her juvenilia, Charlotte also used only male narrators. It is worth noting that Anne's Agnes Grey, the narrator of her own story, addresses the reader on at least two occasions, in chapters 17 and 18. Charlotte's Jane Eyre is famous for speaking directly to her "Reader" throughout.

Recent critics have also pointed out that Anne's novel is a much more realistic depiction of what a governess's life is like than *Jane Eyre*. Jane has only one young child in her care, compared to the several in Agnes's charge. Adèle Varens, Jane's pupil, the daughter of Rochester's former mistress, certainly has faults, but she is affectionate toward Jane, under whose care her behavior improves. Because teaching Adèle takes relatively little of Jane's time, she has the leisure to draw, think, and get to know Rochester. Agnes's job, by contrast, is exhausting and not at all personally fulfilling. Her first job presents her with children whose faults range from bullying to sadism, from mischief to deceit. When she tries to discipline the children, their mother prevents her from doing so, yet after some months Agnes is dismissed for not improving them sufficiently. In her second position, Agnes is expected to teach the daughters of an upper-class family only those things that will improve their chances for marrying well, and to force Latin grammar into the minds of their sons who have no interest in learning. At Thornfield, Jane has to listen to the nasty remarks about governesses made by Blanche Ingram, a house-party guest with whom Rochester flirts in order to make Jane jealous. Jane, however, unlike Agnes, is not treated like a nonentity either by her employer or by the servants.

In Charlotte's third novel, *Shirley*, one of the two heroines asserts that to know if a man is truly good, "we watch him, and see him kind to animals, to little children, to poor people."[9] *Agnes Grey* may also have suggested this idea to Charlotte. One of the ways in which Anne's deeply felt religion makes itself clear in her first novel is in its assertion that all life is God-given and therefore of value. The young son of Agnes's

Facsimile of the Title-Page of the First Edition, which was issued, together with 'Wuthering Heights,' in three volumes, 'Wuthering Heights' forming Volumes 1 and 2.

AGNES GREY.

A NOVEL,

BY

ACTON BELL,

VOL. III.

LONDON:

THOMAS CAUTLEY NEWBY, PUBLISHER,
72, MORTIMER St., CAVENDISH Sq.

———

1847.

Although the title page of this first edition of *Agnes Grey* says "Vol. III," Anne's novel in its entirety makes up this volume. Anne's debut novel was published together in a triple-decker with her sister Emily's sole novel, *Wuthering Heights*, which comprised volumes I and II.

first employer takes pleasure in torturing birds. When Agnes takes extreme steps to prevent him, his mother objects, saying, "You seem to have forgotten . . . that the creatures were all created for our convenience."[10]

Anne's recent biographer Nick Holland notes a passage in *Agnes Grey* that is unlike anything else either in her own novels or in those of her sisters. The eponymous heroine describes herself as she imagines her charges think of her, and in doing so, she summarizes what she believes to be her main attributes both as a governess and as a human being:

> Miss Grey was a queer creature: she never flattered, and did not praise them half enough; but whenever she did speak favourably of them, or anything belonging to them, they could be quite sure her approbation was sincere. She was very obliging, quiet, and peaceable in the main, but there were some things that put her out of temper: they did not much care for that, to be sure, but still it was better to keep her in tune; as when she was in a good humour she would talk to them, and be very agreeable and amusing sometimes, in her way; which was quite different to mamma's, but still very well for a change. She had her own opinions on every subject, and kept steadily to them—very tiresome opinions they often were; as she was always thinking of what was right and what was wrong, and had a strange reverence for matters connected with religion, and an unaccountable liking to good people.[11]

(Note that Anne uses the descriptive term "queer creature" to describe not only Agnes Grey but also, presumably, herself. Attentive readers of this book may remember the adjective "queer" as the same one big sister Charlotte used to describe

Anne on the occasion of the children's choosing soldiers from among those Patrick Brontë gave Branwell in 1826!)

In some ways, Anne's novel shows her not only the most religiously focused of her sisters but also the most feminist. *Agnes Grey* is striking both in its assertion that a woman can be successful without a husband and in depicting a love interest who has nothing of the romantic hero about him. Agnes's mother, a much more admirable character than her spend-thrift husband, tells Mr. Grey that "it's no matter whether [our daughters] get married or not: we can devise a thousand honest ways of making a livelihood."[12] Even after Anne meets the man she will marry, the clergyman Mr. Weston, she parts

ANNE'S DISAPPOINTMENT IN LOVE

Just as Charlotte had a deep love interest that did not culminate in marriage but left an indelible mark on her fiction, so, seemingly, did Anne. In August 1839, William Weightman arrived at the parsonage as a new assistant curate to Patrick Brontë. According to a 2016 biography of Anne, Charlotte found him physically attractive and developed an infatuation with him, which he did not reciprocate. He and Anne, however, seem to have been mutually attracted. Anne is believed to have modeled the character of Reverend Weston—an assistant curate—in *Agnes Grey* on Weightman, with one striking difference: While Weightman was a good-looking man, Weston is described as plain. This discrepancy seems attributable to Anne's interest in emphasizing the character's spiritual depth and kindness. In September 1842, Weightman caught cholera from a patient in Haworth while paying a sick call. He died shortly thereafter. "Anne Brontë's world, and her writing, would never be the same again."[13]

from him in order to join her mother in founding a school. Mr. Weston's attractions are unlike those of Rochester or Heathcliff. Agnes is attracted to him not because she wants a master to submit to but because of his devotion to the gospel of God's love, which he employs to help the poor. Before Agnes does marry, she has become self-supporting by running the school with her mother. After her mother becomes a widow, Mrs. Grey refuses to move in with her daughters, "saying she could now afford to employ an assistant, and would continue the school until she could purchase an annuity sufficient to maintain her in comfortable lodgings."[14] Only in her last novel, *Villette*, did Charlotte come close to depicting a heroine as independent as the women in *Agnes Grey*.

The Tenant of Wildfell Hall: A Revolutionary Novel

When *Agnes Grey* was finally published two months after *Jane Eyre*, it came out as the third of three volumes, following the two comprising *Wuthering Heights*. Among the signs of publisher Thomas Newby's sloppy job in producing the triple-decker is the fact that the title is misspelled as "*Anges Grey*" on six pages. Nonetheless, Anne chose to remain with Newby for her second novel. When Newby released *The Tenant of Wildfell Hall* in the summer of 1848, Anne became the first of the sisters to have a second novel published.

Although Anne's second novel is rooted in her own experience, the heroine, Helen Huntingdon, is not based on Anne herself. The novel tells the story of Helen's decision to flee with her son from her debauched and unfaithful husband, Arthur. Anne appears to have based Arthur Huntingdon and his social circle on her observations of the goings-on at Thorp Green, the home of her second employers, the Robinsons, where Branwell served as tutor to young Edmund Robinson.

In Anne's diary paper of July 1845, she writes, "I am only just escaped from [Thorp Green] . . . during my stay I have had some very unpleasant and undreamt of experience of human nature."[15] Shortly thereafter, Branwell was dismissed when his inappropriate involvement with Mrs. Robinson became known. After Mr. Robinson's death, it slowly dawned on Branwell that the widowed Mrs. Robinson had no plans to marry him. The entire Brontë family watched as this talented young man deadened his pain by drinking to excess and taking drugs. One of the moral lessons that Anne's novel drives home is that boys, like girls, need to be brought up to live lives of discipline and duty. There is nothing cute about introducing a toddler to drink to keep him from becoming a sissy, as happens with the Huntingdons' young son.

If Branwell was the real-life model for Huntingdon and his debauched friends, Helen appears to have been based on the wife of a churchman from a nearby town who visited the Haworth parsonage in the autumn of 1840 and the spring of 1847. Charlotte wrote Ellen Nussey about each of those visits. In the first, the distraught woman described to Mr. Brontë "her wretched husband's drunken, extravagant, profligate habits." Despite the fact that according to English law of the time, it was illegal for a woman to leave her husband, the Reverend Brontë advised the woman "to leave him for ever."[16] The abused wife appears not to have done so, however, since on her second visit to the parsonage she reported how her husband had left her and their two children penniless "to disease and total destitution" in a boardinghouse in Manchester.[17]

While many reviewers loudly objected to Anne's choice of subject matter, enough readers were interested to cause a second edition of *The Tenant of Wildfell Hall* to be printed. In her preface to the second edition, Anne explained herself:

> My object in writing the following pages, was not simply
> to amuse the Reader, neither was it to gratify my own
> taste, nor yet to ingratiate myself with the Press and
> the Public: I wished to tell the truth, for truth, always
> conveys its own moral to those who are able to receive
> it . . . . O Reader! if there were less of this delicate
> concealment of facts . . . there would be less of sin and
> misery to the young of both sexes who are left to wring
> their bitter knowledge from experience.[18]

Some scholars have recently pointed out that part of Anne's
purpose in writing the novel was to correct what she perceived
to be troubling messages in her sisters' novels. Close study of
The Tenant of Wildfell Hall shows that, while borrowing some
features of *Wuthering Heights*, Anne comments on and criti-
cizes elements both of that novel and of *Jane Eyre*.

The most obvious—and least meaningful—comparison
between *Tenant* and *Wuthering Heights* can be found in the
initials of the two houses. Just as Mr. Lockwood comes as a
tenant to Wuthering Heights, so Helen Huntingdon, having
fled her husband's home, comes as a tenant to Wildfell Hall,
a house owned by her brother. With her is her young son,
also named Arthur. Having no legal right to the custody
of her child, she hides her identity by using the pseudonym
Mrs. Graham. Although Isabella flees her abusive husband in
Wuthering Heights, Emily Brontë does not examine Isabella's
life during her thirteen years of self-imposed exile in the south
of England with her son, Linton Heathcliff.

A second comparison is the Chinese box style of narration
of the two novels. In *Wuthering Heights*, Lockwood's narration encloses Nelly Dean's, which encloses contributions from
other narrators. The primary narrator of *The Tenant of Wildfell
Hall* is Gilbert Markham, who tells Helen's story in the form

of a letter to his brother-in-law. Embedded within his letter is Helen Huntingdon's private diary. After Arthur Huntingdon dies, Gilbert Markham eventually marries Helen.

It seems possible, maybe even likely, that among Anne's clear goals in her second novel was to suggest that the attraction readers felt for stormy, manipulative, and bullying heroes like Rochester and Heathcliff was misplaced. Like Isabella, who marries Heathcliff despite being warned not to, Helen allows her physical attraction to Arthur Huntingdon to overcome her aunt's advice to stay away from him. She thinks that she will be able to reform him once they are married. Instead, she discovers that her reforming instincts are no match for the dissolute behavior of her husband and his friends. Among Huntingdon's most sinister friends is Walter Hargrave, who tries to convince Helen to live with him. He argues that to do so would be morally justified, since he would protect her and young Arthur from Huntingdon's abuse. In presenting Hargrave's arguments, Anne may be commenting on Rochester's pleas to Jane to live as his mistress. In giving several thorough villains surnames that begin with "H," including Hargrave and Huntingdon, Anne may be reacting to the several attractive villains—Heathcliff, Hindley, and Hareton—in *Wuthering Heights* whose names also start with that letter.

Anne seems to have objected strongly to Emily's depiction of violence in *Wuthering Heights* for being both too gory and too unrealistic. A case in point is the passage where Isabella reports to Nelly how Heathcliff attacked Hindley with his "sharp, cannibal teeth." When Hindley responds by attacking Heathcliff with his knife, Heathcliff grabs it and draws blood from "an artery, or a large vein."[19] Not yet satisfied, he throws Hindley to the ground, steps on him, and bangs his head on the floor, stopping only to catch his breath. Heathcliff has

Joseph clean up the blood. Although Hindley is described as "sitting, deadly sick" the following morning, there is no way he could have survived such a brutal attack. By contrast, when Anne paints a violent scene in *Tenant*, she is careful to be more realistic. Markham describes the "feeling of savage satisfaction" he gets from the effects of his attack on Frederick Lawrence, whom he mistakes for Helen's lover and therefore a rival.[20] Even though Lawrence ends up on "grass, sodden with rain,"[21] rather than having Markham bash his head against flagstones, it takes him a long time to recover from the attack.

In *Tenant*, the only thoroughly positive male-female relationship is between Helen and her protective and supportive brother, Frederick. Anne may have intended to contrast this wholesome sibling relationship with Emily's depiction of possible half siblings whose feelings for one another border on incest.

Like *Jane Eyre* and *Wuthering Heights*, *The Tenant of Wildfell Hall* ends with a marriage that is a second one for one member of the couple. We know that Jane and Rochester are meant to live happily ever after. Many critics believe that the marriage between Hareton Earnshaw and young Catherine, widow of the sickly Linton Heathcliff, is also meant to restore a sense of order to the world by bringing together the Lintons and Earnshaws and their property. Anne seems to have a more jaundiced view of the prospects for Helen as the wife of Markham. He clearly shares the hot temper, arrogance, and domineering nature that also characterize Heathcliff and Rochester. While many critics see him as learning to master these traits in the course of the novel, others are troubled by the casual manner in which he makes use of Helen's private diary for purposes she never agreed to. In fact, when she entrusts the diary to him, she relies on him not to "breathe a word of what it tells you to any living being."[22] Nonetheless, he conveys the entirety of the diary to his brother-in-law Halford, since "I know you would not be satisfied with an abbreviation of the contents."[23]

Earlier in the novel, Huntingdon tries to control Helen through unauthorized use of her diary. He learns as a result that she plans to leave him and to support herself and her son by selling her paintings. Huntingdon's response is to burn her painting materials and take away her money and jewels. Thanks to her brother's help, she is able to resume her painting in a new studio at Wildfell Hall. In having Markham also make unauthorized use of the diary, Anne may be indicating her fear that marriage robs women of control of their lives. As one critic says, Markham's "nature is the same as that which produced the domestic hell from which his future wife fled, and she finally appears to marry a man as capable of mistreating her as her first husband."[24]

"Currer" and "Acton" Travel to London

Charlotte and Anne clearly did not admire each other's novels. The thought that publishers and readers might believe that all the sisters' novels were the work of a single author would have been equally troubling to both of them. In July 1848 the realization that such a claim was being publicized on both sides of the Atlantic led the oldest and youngest sisters to make a joint hurried trip to London. Their purpose was to erase any doubt that each sister was responsible for her work only.

The impetus for the trip was unscrupulous behavior on the part of Thomas Newby, Anne's publisher. In order to bolster sales of *The Tenant of Wildfell Hall*, Newby was circulating the false story both in England and in America that "to the best of his belief" (as Charlotte wrote her school friend Mary Taylor),

In the summer of 1848, Charlotte and Anne met with Charlotte's publisher, George Murray Smith (*seen here*), to discuss the identity of the Brontë authors. The meeting marked the beginning of a close friendship between Charlotte and George. For her novel *Villette*, Charlotte is said to have modeled Dr. John Graham Bretton—with whom the protagonist, Lucy Snowe, falls in unrequited love—on Smith.

the very successful *Jane Eyre, Wuthering Heights, Agnes Grey,* and the forthcoming *Tenant of Wildfell Hall* "were all the production of one writer."[25] Charlotte and Anne quickly arranged to take the overnight train from Yorkshire to London in order to present themselves to their respective publishers. Emily had no interest in making the trip and stayed at home.

Years later, George Smith remembered how surprised he was to receive "two rather quaintly dressed little ladies, pale-faced and anxious looking." They established their identity by presenting him "with a letter addressed, in my own hand-writing, to 'Currer Bell, Esqu.'"[26] With that visit, described both in Smith's memoir and Charlotte's letter to Mary Taylor, a friend from Roe Head School, Charlotte began warm friendships with both George Smith, her publisher, and W. S. Williams, her editor. All we know of the visit to Newby comes from the final sentence of Charlotte's letter to Mary: "We saw Newby—but of him more another [time]."[27] If Charlotte did describe the confrontation with Newby in another letter, it has not been found.

We do know, however, that Emily was not pleased when she learned what had taken place at the meeting with Charlotte's publishers. On July 31, 1848, Charlotte wrote W. S. Williams:

> Permit me to caution you not to speak of my sisters when you write to me—I mean do not use the word in the plural. "Ellis Bell" will not endure to be alluded to under any other appellation than the "nom de plume." I committed a grand error in betraying <her> "his" identity to you and Mr. Smith—it was inadvertent—the words "we are three sisters" escaped me before I was aware—I regretted the avowal the moment I had made

it; I regret it bitterly now, for I find it is against every feeling and intention of "Ellis Bell."[28]

Ten months later, Charlotte was the only one of the "three sisters" still living.

Marriage and a Mission: Shaping the Family's Literary Reputation

When Currer and Acton Bell arrived in London from Yorkshire on a Saturday morning in July 1848, they knew they would need to find a hotel room. They had, after all, traveled overnight, and before seeking out the offices of their respective publishers, they would have to freshen up and change clothes. The only hotel Charlotte knew of was the Chapter Coffee House, where she and Emily had stayed with their father before their departure for the Pensionnat Heger in Brussels in 1842. They never suspected that they might be exposed in their London lodgings to tuberculosis pathogens, nor that Anne, "perhaps the most amiable and affable of all the Brontës," unwittingly became the carrier who "brought home the infection which killed Branwell and Emily before her."[1]

There was, therefore, no sense of a deathwatch in the parsonage after Charlotte and Anne returned from London. Although Branwell's decline continued, no one—not even his physician—suspected that he had become ill with tuberculosis. Only thirty-one at the time of his death on September 24, Branwell had not been deeply involved in his sisters' lives for many years. A few days after the funeral, Charlotte wrote her editor, W. S. Williams, "I do not weep from a sense of bereavement—there is no prop withdrawn, no consolation torn away, no dear companion lost—but for the wreck of talent, the ruin of promise, the untimely dreary extinction of what might have been a burning and a shining light."[2] Nonetheless, Charlotte had been sufficiently affected by the death of her childhood companion that she left it to Emily and Anne to make preparations for the funeral. Had she been feeling stronger, she might have noticed a decline in her sisters' health.

Strong in mind if not in body until the end, Emily went about her daily routines, even feeding her dogs on the night preceding her own death from tuberculosis. Until midday on December 19, 1848, she refused to consult a doctor or take medication. By that time there was nothing the doctor could do, and she died hours later at the age of thirty. The following day, Charlotte wrote W. S. Williams, "Yesterday Emily Jane Brontë died in the arms of those who loved her . . . The last three months—ever since my brother's death seem to us like a long, terrible dream. We look for support to God—and thus far he mercifully enables us to maintain our self-control in the midst of affliction whose bitterness none of us could have calculated on."[3]

In early January a physician who specialized in treating tuberculosis visited the parsonage and confirmed that it was only a matter of time before Anne, too, would die. Unlike Emily, Anne agreed to try all sorts of medical interventions, but none proved effective. Several of Anne's poems had recently been published in *Fraser's Magazine*, and Anne continued to write despite her decline. In January 1849, she began a poem with the words, "A dreadful darkness closes in." In early April Anne wrote to Charlotte's friend Ellen Nussey that her real regret at the thought of dying young was that she had "lived to so little purpose": "I have no horror of death . . . But I wish it would please God to spare me . . . because I long to do some

Anne Brontë's grave site at St. Mary's churchyard in Scarborough. Note the mistake in the headstone, which says Anne died "aged 28," when in fact she was 29. Charlotte had previously paid to have several other errors on the headstone corrected, but this one remained. The Brontë Society erected a new plaque in 2011 to ensure that visitors over the years to come would be able to decipher the original tombstone, which weather and erosion had rendered illegible in some places.

good in the world before I leave it. I have many schemes in my head . . . humble and limited indeed—but still I should not like them all to come to nothing . . . . But God's will be done."[4]

Anne would be the only Brontë to die away from Haworth. Although her time as governess to the Robinsons had upset her in many ways, Anne had always enjoyed the summers she spent with her employers' family in Scarborough, a popular seaside resort town in northeastern England. In January Mr. Brontë had recorded the specialist's remark "that change of place and climate, could prove beneficial only in the early stages of consumption."[5] Nonetheless, Anne convinced Charlotte that a change of scene might improve her condition. On May 28, Anne died in Scarborough, in the company of Charlotte and Ellen Nussey. She was twenty-nine years old. Charlotte arranged for her burial there to spare her father the pain of witnessing the burial of yet another child.

A few days later, Charlotte wrote to W. S. Williams, comparing her reaction to her sisters' deaths and summarizing her terrible sense of loss: "I let Anne go to God and felt He had a right to her I could hardly let Emily go—I wanted to hold her back then—and I want her back hourly now . . . . They are both gone—and so is poor Branwell—and papa has now me only—the weakest—puniest—least promising of his six children—Consumption has taken the whole five."[6] In another letter she reflected on what the year had brought: "A year ago—had a prophet warned me how I should stand in June 1849—how stripped and bereaved—had he foretold the autumn, the winter, the spring of sickness and suffering to be gone through—I should have thought—this can never be endured. It is over. Branwell—Emily—Anne are gone like dreams—gone as Maria and Elizabeth went twenty years ago. One by one I have watched them fall asleep on my arm—and closed their glazed eyes—I have seen them buried one by one—and—thus far—God has upheld me. From my heart I thank Him."[7]

A Novel Completed in Mourning: *Shirley*

The illnesses and deaths of Charlotte's siblings had kept her from making much progress on her new novel. Preparing to write the book, which is set during the period of the Luddite movement, involved a lot of historical research. The Luddites were groups of workers who, from about 1811 to 1816, reacted to the Industrial Revolution by destroying the new machines that were costing them their jobs. They also threatened the lives of employers who installed such machines. Charlotte had drafted a good chunk of the book before Branwell's death. Now she sensed that throwing herself back into her writing would help her recover from her terrible losses. On different occasions in the summer of 1849, she wrote W. S. Williams, "Labour must be the cure, not sympathy—Labour is the only radical cure for rooted sorrow,"[8] and "my work is my best companion."[9] Charlotte also put this sentiment into the mouth of one of the novel's two heroes, Robert Moore, who tells Shirley, one of the two heroines, "So long as I can be active, so long as I can strive, so long, in short, as my hands are not tied, it is impossible for me to be depressed."[10]

According to Elizabeth Gaskell, Charlotte "had nearly finished the second volume of her tale when Branwell died—after him Emily—after her Anne; the pen, laid down when there were three sisters living and loving, was taken up when one alone remained. Well might she call the first chapter that she wrote after this 'The Valley of the Shadow of Death.'"[11] Gaskell also informs us that Charlotte drew on her memories of Emily in creating the portrait of Shirley. One episode in which Shirley is bitten by a rabid dog, for example, is based on an experience of Emily's. After being similarly attacked, Emily took "one of Tabby's red-hot Italian irons to sear the bitten place, and telling no one, till the danger was wellnigh over."[12]

Shirley is a flawed novel. The heiress heroine for whom the book is named does not appear for many chapters, and the man she marries appears only two-thirds of the way into the novel. The book focuses primarily on a second heroine, Caroline Helstone, who is being raised by her uncle, the Reverend Matthewson Helstone. Nonetheless, among the things to admire in *Shirley* are several passages in which Charlotte explores the meaning of life for unmarried women. In one, for example, Caroline wonders, " . . . half a century of existence may lie before me. How am I to occupy it? What am I to do to fill the interval of time which spreads between me and the grave . . . Probably I shall be an old maid . . . I shall never marry. What was I created for, I wonder? Where is my place in the world?"[13] Interestingly enough, Mary Taylor felt her school friend Charlotte did not go far enough in her critique of a society that left women with nothing to do but "stick to the needle—learn shirt-making and gown-making, and pie-crust making."[14] According to Mary, Charlotte seemed to be saying that only unmarried women need trouble themselves with the idea of a profession to give meaning to their lives. For refusing to state clearly that any woman, married or not, "who works is by that alone better than one who does not," Mary called Charlotte "a coward & a traitor."[15]

A Self-Appointed Literary Executor Creates "the Brontë Myth"

Only three months after Anne's death, Charlotte was able to write W. S. Williams, "The book is now finished . . . .Whatever now becomes of the work—the occupation of writing it has been a boon to me—it took me out of dark and desolate reality to an unreal but happier region."[16] The simple understanding that work helps distract one from grief, however, did not make it any easier for Charlotte to figure out what her next project should be. An attempt to write a new novel with a narrator who told her own story, as Jane Eyre had, failed to gel.

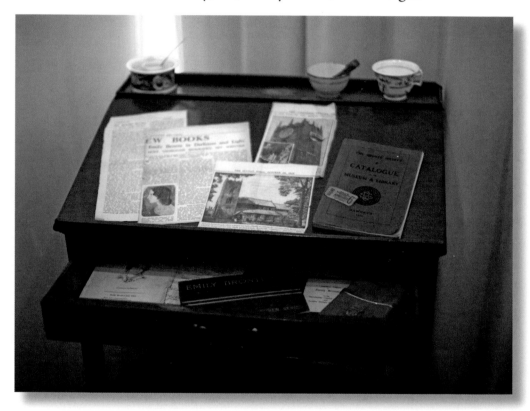

The Brontë Parsonage Museum acquired Charlotte's writing desk in 1944. Emily and Anne had similar portable desks, which, when closed, formed shoebox-sized rectangular cases. The opened desks had slots at the top to hold bottles of ink and storage areas in which the sisters hid all sorts of keepsakes. It is likely that the sisters took their portable desks with them to their teaching and governess positions.

Charlotte's next project turned out not to be a novel at all. When Smith, Elder and Company proposed to put out a new edition of her sisters' work, Charlotte signed on as editor and biographer. For the new edition of *Wuthering Heights*, *Agnes Grey*, and a selection of her sisters' poems, Charlotte wrote three essays: "Biographical Notice of Ellis and Acton Bell," "Editor's Preface to the New Edition of *Wuthering Heights*," and "Prefatory Note to 'Selections from Poems by Ellis Bell.'"

Recent critics have not been kind in judging her efforts or her motives. Although Charlotte claimed in a letter to W. S. Williams, "I would not offer a line to the publication of which my sisters themselves would have objected,"[17] she violated that self-imposed rule in many ways. According to one critic, in editing Emily's poems and novel, Charlotte "had no scruples in modifying her sister's work to take account of what she thought the public would want to read."[18] In editing Anne's work, "Charlotte showed her sister a mixture of maternal care and sisterly jealousy."[19] According to another critic, "As surviving sister, Charlotte was in the position to determine which of Emily's and Anne's works were reprinted and which were not."[20]

Among the executive decisions Charlotte made that affected how her sisters' reputations would develop over the decades to come was to keep *The Tenant of Wildfell Hall* from being reissued. She wrote W. S. Williams in September 1850, "'Wildfell Hall' it hardly seems to me desirable to preserve. The choice of subject in that work is a mistake."[21] As one critic notes, "Had [*Wildfell Hall*] been more widely available, it might have helped generate representations of a new kind of heroine, more spirited and independent."[22]

In editing her sisters' poems for the new edition, Charlotte made some changes—like hiding the Gondal origins of poems—that Emily and Anne would likely have approved. She also made changes that would have enraged them. For example, when Emily describes cornfields as "emerald and scarlet and gold," Charlotte substituted for "scarlet" the pretentious word "vermeil," which Emily is unlikely to have used.[23] Charlotte failed to point out to readers the changes she had made.

Another decision Charlotte made was to change the spelling of Joseph's dialect in *Wuthering Heights*. What resulted from Charlotte's editorial changes has been called a "hit-or-miss mixture of dialect and standard English," which is not nearly the equal of Emily's original.[24] It took many decades for later editors of *Wuthering Heights* to restore Emily's version. Charlotte's discussion of *Wuthering Heights* both in the preface and the biographical essay also does a real injustice to the novel. Her use of the phrase "the interpretation" falsely implies that there is only one way to read the book.[25] Some of her judgments now seem totally erroneous. For example, Charlotte's assessments of Nelly Dean ("a specimen of true benevolence and homely fidelity"), Edgar Linton ("an example of constancy and tenderness"), or Heathcliff ("the single link that connects Heathcliff with humanity is his rudely confessed regard for Hareton Earnshaw") are simply not believable.[26]

In presenting her sisters to the public, Charlotte hid their educational background, which had enabled them to draw on the varied literary sources they had been reading since childhood, and misrepresented the level of their artistry: "Neither Emily nor Anne was learned; they had no thought of filling their pitchers at the well-spring of other minds; they always wrote from the impulse of nature, the dictates of intuition, and from such stores of observation as their limited experience had enabled them to amass."[27] In doing so, she began to create the false impression of the Brontë family literary output that has since come to be known as "the Brontë myth." Charlotte explained that she undertook her task "because I felt it a sacred duty to wipe the dust off their gravestones, and leave their dear names free from soil."[28] What she wrote, however, had the effect of putting up a barrier between her sisters' work and the reading public. As her sisters' self-appointed literary executor, she got to shape their reputations. As one critic has concluded, "One can well imagine that both her sisters would have been infuriated by Charlotte's unwarranted interference in their work; it was on a par with her many attempts to organize them during their lives."[29]

Transforming the Oft-Rejected *The Professor* into *Villette*

With her editorial and biographical work behind her, Charlotte once again began a new novel. In 1851, Smith, Elder's refusal to publish a revised version of *The Professor*, based on her stay a decade earlier in Brussels, prompted Charlotte to use this same experience as the basis for a new novel, titled *Villette*. Many readers and critics believe *Villette* to be her finest achievement. Its heroine, Lucy Snowe, who insists, "I am a rising character,"[30] demonstrates Charlotte's belief that women have the ability to forge their own identities despite the odds.

The writing of *Villette* did not come easily, however. Charlotte's loneliness and concerns about her father's health often overcame her, and she suffered periods of depression that left her unable to work. She wrote to her publisher, George Smith, in November 1851, "If I could always work—time would not be long—nor hours sad to me—but blank and heavy intervals still occur—when power and will are at variance."[31] At the end of the year, she was so ill that writing was out of the question. In March 1852, she wrote her former teacher Margaret Wooler, "For nearly four months now . . . I have not put pen to paper . . . my faculties have been rusting for want of exercise . . . My publisher groans over my long delays."[32]

By the end of October, she had submitted the first two volumes of *Villette*. She wrote George Smith, urging him and W. S. Williams to be honest in their assessment of the novel: "I can hardly tell you how much I hunger to have some opinion besides my own, and how I have sometimes desponded and almost despaired because there was no one to whom to read a line—or of whom to ask a counsel. 'Jane Eyre' was not written under such circumstances, nor were two-thirds of 'Shirley.'"[33] The writers' workshops, of course, had come to an end when her sisters fell ill. The reaction Charlotte received from Smith, Elder was encouraging enough to enable her to complete the third volume within the next month. When the final volume was met with silence, however, Charlotte began to worry that the publisher would reject the novel outright or demand revisions she did not wish to make. While Smith did have misgivings about the novel's ending, he agreed to publish it as is.

Many readers today admire *Villette* precisely because of Charlotte's unwillingness to write a conventional happy ending. The heroine, Lucy Snowe, is another one of Charlotte's motherless women who manages to create an identity, achieve professional satisfaction, and find love. In the end, it is unclear whether the professor, Monsieur Paul Emanuel, with whom Lucy has fallen in love and who loves her in return, dies in a shipwreck en route home from the West Indies. What is clear is that Lucy has found happiness, even in his absence, in running the school he has set up for her: "M. Emanuel was

The death of M. Constantin Héger has excited considerable comment in this country on account of his having been Charlotte Brontë's Brussels schoolmaster and the prototype of Paul Emanuel in "Villette." But M. Héger, who died in Brussels on May 6 at the age of eighty-seven, had numerous claims to consideration as Professor of Latin at the Royal Athénée at Brussels and the friend of three generations of pupils. After fighting in the war of 1830, which secured his country's independence of the Dutch, M. Héger turned his attention to teaching, and for fifty-two years he taught both in the Athénée and at his wife's Pensionnat in the Rue d'Isabelle. M. Héger was a man of high character and profound learning. He leaves behind him one son—Dr. Héger, of Brussels—and three daughters to mourn his loss. Our portrait is from a painting by M. Louis Jambero.

THE LATE M. CONSTANTIN HEGER.

Constantin Heger was Charlotte's tutor in Brussels as well as the object of her affection. *Villette* and *The Professor* were based on her experiences from that time. This obituary of Monsieur Heger appeared in the *Illustrated London News* of June 6, 1896, forty-one years after Charlotte's death.

125

away three years. Reader, they were the three happiest years of my life . . . I commenced my school; I worked—I worked hard."[34] Lucy then describes the storm that imperils his ship, but refuses to say if he ever makes it back to Villette, the fictional town (modeled on Brussels) in the fictional kingdom of Labassecour (modeled on Belgium) in which most of the novel's action takes place.

Who would have expected that the genteel Charlotte Brontë's narrative technique in her last novel would be compared more than a century and a half later to that of a TV drama about gangsters? In 2007, when the HBO series *The Sopranos* aired its final episode, many fans did not know what to make of the final scene, a blackout that refused to tie up loose ends. A reviewer for the *New York Times* compared that ambiguous ending to "the ending of Charlotte Brontë's *Villette*, . . . which she rewrote at the urging of her father so that it's left for the reader to decide whether or not the heroine's true love, M. Paul, dies in a shipwreck."[35] Charlotte would no doubt have been amazed to find her final novel referred to in this context, but the comparison is certainly a tribute to her enduring artistic legacy.

Finding Short-Lived Happiness in an Unlikely Marriage

In late August 1852, Charlotte wrote to her old friend Ellen Nussey that "the Future sometimes appals [sic] me" not because "I am a single woman and likely to remain a single woman—but because I am a lonely woman and likely to be lonely."[36] William Makepeace Thackeray, the author whom Charlotte so admired and who, in turn, had admired *Jane Eyre* on reading it five years earlier, found signs of Charlotte's loneliness throughout *Villette*. He wrote to a friend, who was also reading *Villette*, about what he had deduced by scrutinizing Charlotte's latest novel: "I can read a great deal of her life as I fancy in her book, and see that rather than have fame, rather than any other earthly good or mayhap heavenly one she wants some Tomkins or another to love her and be in love with. But you see she is a little bit of a creature without a penny worth of good looks, . . . buried in the country, and eating up her own heart there, and no Tomkins will come."[37]

Thackeray was only partly right about Brontë. A petite and pleasant—if ordinary-looking—woman in her midthirties, Charlotte had received proposals of marriage from more than one "Tomkins" over the years. In 1839, when she was twenty-two, she rejected a proposal from her friend Ellen's brother Henry. She wrote Ellen that while she found Henry "an amiable and well-disposed man," she lacked "that intense attachment which would make me willing to die for him."[38] In that letter, Charlotte expressed her belief that "ten to one I shall never have the chance again," but she was proven wrong. Only a few months later, she turned down another proposal. Charlotte's second suitor was a visiting Irish clergyman, the Reverend David Pryce, who had met her only once. Charlotte wrote Ellen, "I've heard of love at first sight but this beats all. I leave you to guess what my answer would be—."[39]

In 1851, Charlotte turned down an opportunity to marry James Taylor, an employee of Smith, Elder and Company, who was about to go to India to manage the company's business there. Even though her father approved of Taylor, Charlotte wrote Ellen: "Were I to marry him—my heart would bleed—in pain and humiliation—I could not—could not look up to him—No—if Mr. T—be the only husband Fate offers to me—single I must always remain."[40]

Charlotte probably was in love with someone at Smith, Elder, but that someone was George Smith himself, who was eight years younger than Charlotte. In early 1851, Charlotte discussed her relationship with her publisher in a letter to Ellen: "Were there no vast barrier of age, fortune &c. there is perhaps enough personal regard to make things possible which now are impossible . . . Meantime I am content to have him as a friend . . . ."[41] In November 1853, Charlotte learned that Smith was engaged to be married. Only then did Charlotte accept a proposal that had come to her out of the blue eleven months earlier. In a letter to Ellen, Charlotte described the passionate proposal she received in December 1852 from Arthur Bell Nicholls, her father's curate for the past seven years: "Shaking from head to foot, looking deadly pale, speaking low, vehemently yet with difficulty—he made me for the first time feel what it costs a man to declare affection where he doubts response."[42]

Nicholls had reason to doubt the response. Charlotte's father was irate at his curate's effrontery. Perhaps he believed that an Irish-born clergyman with no fortune was a poor match for his now famous author daughter. Charlotte, too, had no particular regard for Nicholls, who was one of the clergymen she had satirized in *Shirley*. By spring 1854, however, both Mr. Brontë and Charlotte had changed their minds. As Charlotte wrote to George Smith that April, "Various circumstances have led my Father to consent . . ., nor can I deny that my own feelings have been much impressed and changed by the nature and strength of the qualities brought out in the course of his long attachment. I fear I must accuse myself of having formerly done him less than justice."[43] The marriage took place on June 29, 1854. The bride was thirty-eight; the groom, thirty-six.

Charlotte went into her marriage with open eyes. She told Catherine Winkworth, a close friend of Elizabeth Gaskell, of a real difference between herself and Nicholls: "I cannot conceal from myself that he is not intellectual; there are many places into which he could not follow me intellectually."[44] She told her former teacher and employer Margaret Wooler, "The destiny which Providence in His goodness and wisdom seems to offer me will not—I am aware—be generally regarded as brilliant—but I trust <it> I see in it some germs of real happiness."[45] In the event, those germs of happiness barely had time to sprout.

During the couple's honeymoon in Ireland and after their return home, Charlotte found much to love about Nicholls. By November, Charlotte was able to write Wooler, "I have a good, kind, attached husband, and every day makes my own attachment to him stronger."[46] As she approached the six-month anniversary of her marriage, she wrote to Ellen, "He is 'my dear boy' certainly—dearer now than he was six months ago—

WHAT CHARLOTTE BRONTË HAD IN COMMON WITH KATE MIDDLETON

The technical term for the cause of Charlotte's death is *hyperemesis gravidarum*, from the Greek words for excessive vomiting in pregnant women. The same condition afflicted Catherine, Duchess of Cambridge—better known as Kate Middleton, wife of Prince William—during both of her pregnancies. The first medical explanation of the condition, which is much more severe than morning sickness, was made in 1852, only three years before Charlotte's death from it. At that time, it was a common cause of death in pregnancy, but today, when treatment—at least in economically developed countries—is widely available, such deaths are rare.[47]

in three days we shall actually have been married that length of time!"[48]

About two weeks later, however, Charlotte fell ill. Her symptoms led her to suspect that she was pregnant, as she implied in a letter to Ellen in January 1855: "My health has been really very good ever since my return from Ireland till about ten days ago . . . indigestion and continual faint sickness have been my portion ever since. Don't conjecture—dear Nell—for it is too soon yet—though I certainly never before felt as I have done lately."[49] A month later Charlotte assured her friend from girlhood, "I find in my husband the tenderest nurse, the kindest support—the best earthly comfort that ever woman had."[50]

On March 31, 1855, Charlotte died three weeks short of her thirty-ninth birthday. Although the official death certificate cites the cause of death as tuberculosis, scholars today think Charlotte's death was most likely brought about by the severe vomiting that accompanied her pregnancy. A few days after the funeral, the Reverend Brontë wrote Charlotte's friend Elizabeth Gaskell, "The marriage that took place, seem'd to hold forth, long, and bright prospects of happiness, but in the inscrutable providence of God, all our hopes, have ended in disappointment, and our joy <ended> in mourning—."[51]

CHARLOTTE BRONTË'S MALE SURVIVORS: TURNING OVER THE FAMILY'S HISTORY TO OTHERS

What would become of the Brontë story now that the last of the siblings had died? Charlotte had perhaps overstepped in curating the literary reputations of her sisters in the aftermath of their deaths, but who would now shape Charlotte's legacy and present an accurate portrait of the family's history to the many fans of the three author siblings? Many people who had anything to do with the Brontë family now saw an opportunity to become famous because of their association—however limited—with the now famous authors. Others saw simply the opportunity to make some money. One example of someone motivated by both impulses was John Greenwood, the Haworth stationer. Hardly a close friend of the family, he nonetheless represented himself as one. Other Haworth inhabitants with even the slightest connection to the family also embellished their claims to intimacy with the Brontës.

According to Charlotte's last will and testament, however, there would be only one authorized keeper of the family's flame. This document, signed a month and a half before her death, stipulated if she were to die without leaving behind a child, all her property was to be left to her husband, "to be his absolutely and entirely."[1] This meant that he alone held the copyright to all her work. No one could publish Charlotte's letters, for example, without her husband's permission. Arthur Bell Nicholls would become what his biographer would much later call "a conscientious preserver of the sisters' literary reputation."[2]

The Survivors' Attempt to Keep Private Matters Off-Limits to Public Eyes

In the months following Charlotte's death, the Reverend Brontë and Arthur Bell Nicholls were disturbed to see articles filled with misinformation appear in the popular press. Both men believed that to respond to such pieces would merely focus more attention on them. Ellen Nussey, however, urged them to ask Charlotte's friend Elizabeth Gaskell, already a well-known and popular novelist, to write a biography that would set the record straight. In 1855, therefore, Mr. Brontë wrote Gaskell that "having reason to think that, some may venture to write her life, who will be ill qualified for the undertaking, I can see no better plan . . . than to apply to some established Author, to write a brief account of her life—and to make some remarks on her works—You, seem to me, to be the best qualified, for doing what I wish should be done."[3] The Reverend Brontë did not know that Gaskell had already formed a negative opinion of him. He later wrote her that he had "freely . . . spoken to you—in order that in your work, you may insert such facts, as may counteract, <and>`any/false statements, that may have been made, or might be made, respecting me, or mine."[4] His trust was misplaced.

When Gaskell accepted his proposal, the Reverend Brontë started the ball rolling by sending her a letter describing his

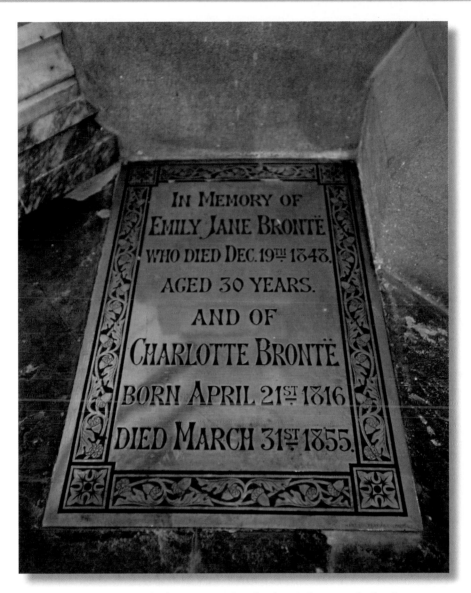

This brass memorial plaque marks the burial spot of Charlotte and Emily Brontë. The crypt containing their remains, as well as those of their father, mother, aunt, and brother, was sealed by the Reverend Patrick Brontë's successor, the Reverend John Wade. In 2010, parishioners of Haworth Parish Church announced a fundraising drive for refurbishment, in hopes of opening the crypt to future visitors.

background and his children's lives. Gaskell continued her research by collecting as many of Charlotte's letters—to Ellen Nussey, Margaret Wooler, and George Smith—as she could, and by interviewing people who had known her. Some of these, including John Greenwood, the Haworth stationer, claimed a closer connection to Charlotte than they really had. For details about Charlotte's life, Gaskell relied heavily on Ellen Nussey, whose opinions she accepted without question. Gaskell made little attempt to get the perspectives of Charlotte's father or widower. To her credit, she did travel to Brussels to interview Monsieur and Madame Heger. The latter refused to meet Gaskell, but the former described his teaching philosophy and produced some examples of essays Emily and Charlotte had written for him. He also gave her selected paragraphs from Charlotte's correspondence with him.

Gaskell had no interest in publishing even expurgated sections from Charlotte's love letters to Heger, however. A few years earlier, Charlotte claimed to have written the "Biographical Notice" of her sisters because she "felt it a sacred duty to wipe the dust off their gravestones, and leave their dear names free from soil."[5] Now Gaskell felt it was her responsibility to "make the world . . . honour the woman as much as they have admired the writer."[6] She thought the way to do this was to depict Charlotte as the embodiment of purity, whose behavior would never raise an eyebrow. According to Gaskell, whatever coarseness reviewers had found in Charlotte's books resulted from the circumstances of her upbringing. One reviewer of Gaskell's *The Life of Charlotte Brontë*, which Smith, Elder published in March 1857, summarized the biographer's point of view: "Charlotte Brontë's . . . home held a monster whom the strong ties of an inordinate family affection constrained her to love and care for and find excuses for. Whatever exten-

In recent years, *Masterpiece Classic* has mounted television
miniseries productions based on three classic novels by
Charlotte's biographer, Elizabeth Gaskell (*pictured here*): *Cranford*,
North and South, and *Wives and Daughters*.

uation can be found for . . . outrages on propriety . . . the home and the neighbourhood of Charlotte Brontë certainly furnish; she wrote in ignorance of offending public opinion."[7]

Reverend Brontë's inclination was to say nothing about Gaskell's misrepresentations of him. Only when it became apparent that Gaskell had to make other changes in the book to protect herself from libel lawsuits did Brontë finally ask her to change some of her more outrageous claims about him. He warned her of something of which every biographer should be aware: "It is dangerous, to give credence hastily, to informants—some may tell the truth, whilst others from various motives may greedily, invent and propagate falsehoods."[8]

Even in its third and final edition, Gaskell's *Life of Charlotte Brontë* is flawed. Her description of Patrick Brontë remained unfair. She emphasized the sad episodes of the children's early years and played down their exuberant involvement in joint writing projects. Nor does the biography give any sense of Charlotte's adult sense of humor. Gaskell was unaware of Branwell Brontë's publications and focused only on his addictions and disruptive behavior. She refused to let her readers know about Charlotte's obsession with Monsieur Heger. She relied too heavily on Charlotte's and Ellen's biased assessments of Emily's and Anne's achievements. Nonetheless, the book found a mass audience. Even people who had never read the Brontës' works were interested in their lives. From 1857 on, it was hard to read the sisters' poems and novels without searching for biographical references. Some people even began confusing the sisters with their characters.

If Charlotte's "Biographical Notice" gave birth to what is called the "Brontë myth," claiming her sisters' lives explained their literary works, Gaskell's biography extended that myth to Charlotte and spread it far and wide. The biography remains an important source of information about the Brontës, but readers are cautioned to seek out other biographies with different points of view. By intriguing readers with stories about the Brontës' lives in the parsonage, Gaskell's *Life of Charlotte Brontë* also turned Haworth into the major site of literary tourism that it remains today.

Charlotte's Literary Remains

In 1851, when Smith, Elder declined to publish her first novel, *The Professor*, Charlotte humorously but resolutely refused to entrust the manuscript to the firm. As she wrote to George Smith, it would not be fair to the manuscript, since "with slips of him you might light an occasional cigar—or you might remember to lose him some day," or some employee might "consign him to the repositories of waste paper." Instead, Charlotte took "this martyrized M.S." and "locked him up . . . in a cupboard by himself." Recognizing that "few . . . have earned an equal distinction" of having a manuscript rejected nine times, she compared her "feelings towards it" to "those of a doting parent towards an idiot child."[9] Announcements of its death, however, turned out to be premature.

The Brontë materials Elizabeth Gaskell took away with her after her July 1856 visit to the parsonage included the manuscript of *The Professor* and a twenty-page marked manuscript drafted in pencil, dated November 27, 1853. After reading Charlotte's much-rejected first novel, Gaskell felt it should remain unpublished. To release it now would only confirm the negative assessment of Charlotte's literary skills held by some. Nonetheless, Smith, Elder and Company, which had turned down the novel more than once, now wanted to take advantage of the interest Charlotte's death had generated. Arthur Bell Nicholls agreed to edit the manuscript in preparation for publication. The market considerations that had led the publishers to reject the novel before—the likelihood that *The Professor* would fail to sell many copies—now led them to promote it, since anything by the now acclaimed author would surely sell well. As it turned out, *The Professor*, published in June 1857, disappointed the publishers' hopes for substantial sales. The most reviewers could say about it was that it proved how much Charlotte's skills had grown over the course of her brief career.

Despite the lackluster response to this posthumous publication, public interest in the Brontës remained strong. In 1859 George Smith wrote Nicholls asking for permission to publish, in a new magazine he was about to launch, the two chapters of the novel Charlotte never finished. Nicholls agreed, and the first issue of Smith's *Cornhill Magazine* included the fragments of *Emma*, the working title. Like other Brontë novels, *Emma* is the story of a motherless girl in a boarding school. Like Heathcliff's in *Wuthering Heights*, the heroine's appearance suggests she might be of mixed racial background.

Why Charlotte gave her last, if incompletely drawn, heroine the same given name as Emma Woodhouse, the eponymous protagonist of Jane Austen's popular 1815 novel *Emma*, is unclear. We know that Austen's *Emma* was one of three novels by that author that Charlotte's editor George Smith sent to her in a parcel of twenty books in the spring of 1850. We also know from Charlotte's letter of April 12, 1850, to W. S. Williams, the literary advisor to Smith, Elder and Co., that she was not a big fan of *Emma*.

> I have likewise read one of Miss Austen's works Emma—read it with interest and with just the right degree of admiration which the Miss Austen herself would have thought sensible and suitable—anything

like warmth or enthusiasm; anything energetic, poignant, heartfelt, is utterly out of place in commending these works: all such demonstration the authoress would have met with a well-bred sneer, would have calmly scorned as outré and extravagant.[10]

eponymous
Referring to being the person or thing after whom something is named.

Whatever Charlotte's reason for bestowing the name she did on her title character, the fragment was published along with an introduction by novelist William Makepeace Thackeray. According to Thackeray, six months into their marriage, Charlotte enlisted her husband in a variation of the sisters' writers' workshop: "One evening, at the close of 1854, as Charlotte Nicholls sat with her husband by the fire, listening to

FLESHING OUT CHARLOTTE BRONTË'S *EMMA*

Toward the end of the twentieth century and at the beginning of the twenty-first, two fleshed-out expansions of Charlotte Brontë's fragment *Emma* were published. The first, from 1980, appeared anonymously, as *An Emma by Charlotte Brontë and "Another Lady."* According to rumors, the other lady was English author Elizabeth Goudge (1900–1984), whose novel *The Little White Horse* (1946) was one of the few books that J. K. Rowling credits as having had a direct influence on the Harry Potter series. A more recent expansion, *Emma Brown*, came out in 2003, the last book by Irish author Clare Boylan (1948–2006). In addition, in 2002 *The Day I Finished Off Charlotte Brontë*, a radio drama by London-based artist and writer Charlotte Cory, was broadcast. It imagines the story of nine-year-old Allaetetia who, in the 1960s, decides to complete Brontë's unfinished novel.[11]

the howling of the wind about the house, she suddenly said to her husband, 'If you had not been with me, I must have been writing now.' She then ran upstairs, and brought down, and read aloud, the beginning of a new tale. When she had finished, her husband remarked, 'The critics will accuse you of repetition.' She replied, 'Oh! I shall alter that. I always begin two or three times before I can please myself.' But it was not to be. The trembling little hand was to write no more."[12] Had Charlotte lived longer, perhaps Arthur would have proven an effective sounding board for her works in progress.

The Transmission of Copyright

When Charlotte described to George Smith her complicated feelings about her upcoming marriage, she singled out with relief the relationship that had developed between Nicholls and her father: "On one feature in the marriage I can dwell with unmingled satisfaction—with a certainty of being right. It takes nothing from the attention I owe to my Father. I am not to leave him—my 'future' husband consents to come here—thus <he> 'Papa' secures by the step—a devoted and reliable assistant in his old age."[13] Charlotte did not live to see how right her prediction proved to be.

Less than two months after Charlotte's death, the Reverend Brontë prepared his own will. In it he left all but 70 pounds to his "beloved and esteemed Son-in-Law . . . for his own absolute benefit."[14] Six years later, on June 7, 1861, the Reverend Brontë died at the age of eighty-four. Though his ill health had caused his daughters much concern, none of them reached half their father's age.

During the six years following Charlotte's death, Arthur Bell Nicholls carried out all of Reverend Brontë's clerical duties. Most people expected that Nicholls would be appointed

Charlotte Brontë's marriage to Arthur Bell Nicholls (*pictured*) was reenacted in the 2016 BBC Two production *Being the Brontës*, with Mark Aiken as Nicholls and Sophie Trott as Charlotte Brontë.

his father-in-law's replacement. The church trustees decided, however, to give the position to a wealthier man. Perhaps they hoped the new man would be able to pay for repairs to the church and the parsonage that the trustees had been responsible for during Brontë's long period of service. In any case, Nicholls found himself facing immediate homelessness. The parsonage would now be turned over to Brontë's successor. He rapidly packed up all of the Brontë possessions and took them with him to his ancestral home in Ireland. For the remaining forty-five years of his life, he supported himself there as a farmer. In 1864, nine years after Charlotte's death, he married a cousin, Mary Anna Bell, whom Charlotte had met on her honeymoon in Ireland. The new Mrs. Nicholls respected his devotion to the Brontës. Only after Nicholls's death, in 1906, did she begin to sell items her husband had treasured. Financial need left her no choice.

Arthur Bell Nicholls's own financial need was perhaps the reason why, on two occasions in 1895, he turned over the rights to all the Brontë letters and manuscripts to Clement King Shorter, in exchange for some hundreds of pounds. Ever since Charlotte's death, Nicholls had fought off repeated requests from Ellen Nussey for permission to publish all of her correspondence with Charlotte, which Nussey—but not the law of the land—considered to be hers. Nussey had circumvented Nicholls's hold on the copyright in every legal way she could. Over the years, she had managed without incurring legal difficulty to have excerpts from the letters published, and in 1870, she was able to have a volume of the letters published in the United States, where the copyright of foreign authors would not be protected until more than twenty years later. How frustrated Nussey must have been to discover that after Nicholls had thwarted her publishing aspirations for decades, the newcomer Shorter had succeeded in a mere matter of months to secure the copyright she had so vigorously sought to no avail. Shorter went on to publish two books about Charlotte Brontë and two about the Brontë family, as well as an edited version of Elizabeth Gaskell's *Life of Charlotte Brontë* in 1899.

The Transmission of Brontë Treasures

In a letter to Clement Shorter in the spring of 1904, Mary Nicholls reported that her husband had been busy burning old papers. Clearly, however, Nicholls did not burn everything of value. In the months following Arthur's death in early December 1906, then again in 1914, the auction house Sotheby's put up for bids on behalf of Mary Nicholls some of the Brontë items that her late husband had treasured. The first trove included books from the parsonage as well as some of the tiny manuscripts that the Brontë siblings had produced during their youth, while the second trove included Charlotte's manuscript of her unfinished novel, *Emma*. The two sales brought in over thirteen hundred pounds to the widow. Following Mary Nicholls's death in 1915, a final sale in December 1916, the tenth anniversary of the death of Arthur Bell Nicholls, brought in an additional 173 pounds to her estate.

Among the treasures that eventually made their way from the possession of the Nicholls family, perhaps the most famous is the only known portrait of the three Brontë sisters. According to a niece of Mary Nicholls, the portrait, painted by Branwell Brontë around 1834, when he was only seventeen, was discovered while her aunt was watching an attendant dust some items that had been stored on top of a piece of furniture that was being moved to a different room. This admittedly not great work of art became part of the collection of the National Portrait Gallery in London in 1914. In preparation for the festivities honoring the two hundredth birthday of Charlotte Brontë, the painting underwent scientific tests. Expert analysis of the results revealed that beneath the pillar that separates Anne and Emily, on one side of the painting, from the sole figure of Charlotte on the other side, Branwell had originally sketched himself. He is now believed to have edited himself out of the portrait immediately. As an assistant curator of the exhibition said, "The pillar was added at an early stage, so it appears he painted himself over."[15] The portrait became the centerpiece not only of the National Gallery's exhibit in London but also of the Morgan Library's exhibit in New York.

Into the Twenty-First Century and Beyond: The Brontë Sisters' Enduring Legacy

The Brontë sisters were not the first authors in English literary history to inspire a cult of celebrity. According to a 2016 exhibit at the Folger Shakespeare Library in Washington, DC, "Modern celebrity culture was born in the late eighteenth century when a growing entertainment industry staged popular spectacles and exhibitions that fanned the flames of Shakespeare's early reputation." Literary tourism provided a way for Shakespeare's audiences to feel closer to their beloved playwright, as they visited sites associated with events in the Bard's life. In addition, "aggressive merchandizing of Shakespeare" provided devoted fans with a "ubiquity of souvenirs," from porcelain figures and mass-produced portraits to dolls and other toys. Parodies and modernized versions of the plays were written and produced to make the work seem relevant to the modern day.[1] The Brontë sisters are among other authors since that time who have aroused and sustained that kind of enthusiasm in their readers.

One way to assess the legacy of a writer is to judge the impact his or her work has made on general culture. The impact of the Brontës is truly staggering. Their works continue to inspire not only countless biographies and works

This bronze statue of the three Brontë sisters by Jocelyn Horner (1902–1973) has stood since 1951 in the garden of the Brontë Parsonage Museum, which commissioned it. Charlotte is on the left, Emily in the middle, and Anne on the right.

of criticism but also all sorts of other creative efforts, ranging from literary, musical, dramatic, and cinematic contributions to "high culture," to pop songs, comic routines, and other contributions to popular culture. Catalogues of such Brontë spin-offs fill many pages and are never complete, because more continue to appear all the time. Rather than attempting to provide a comprehensive overview of all the ways in which the Brontë sisters' work continues to inspire new creativity, this chapter will focus on a few of the by-now classic works based on Brontë antecedents and introduce a sample of some of the newest contributions to the field. Not surprisingly, the years leading up to and including the Brontë two-hundredth-birthday celebrations proved particularly fertile ones for new adaptations in a variety of categories.

Twenty-First Century Biographies and Scholarly Works

The first two decades of the twenty-first century saw the publication of important biographies not only of two of the three Brontë sisters—Claire Harman's *Charlottte Brontë: A Fiery Heart*, Nick Holland's *In Search of Anne Brontë*, and Samantha Ellis's *Take Courage: Anne Brontë and the Art of Life*— but also of the sole Brontë spouse—Alan H. Adamson's *Mr. Charlotte Brontë: The Life of Arthur Bell Nicholls*. Perhaps more importantly, an updated, entirely revised collective biography of the members of "one of England's most legendary literary families" was issued. Juliet Barker's *The Brontës: Wild Genius on the Moors: The Story of Three Sisters* received a starred review in *Kirkus Reviews*. Calling it "a massive, almost certainly definitive biography," and "a triumph," the review concludes "it's hard to imagine anyone else ever again getting quite this close to the Brontës."[2]

Readers aged twelve to sixteen have not been overlooked in the run-up to the Brontë bicentennials. *Kirkus Reviews* also gives a starred review to Catherine Reef's *The Brontë Sisters: The Brief Lives of Charlotte, Emily, and Anne*, praising its "solid and captivating look at these remarkable pioneers of modern fiction."[3]

Not quite a biography, but nonetheless an important addition to biographical insights into Charlotte Brontë, the Brontë Society published *Celebrating Charlotte Brontë: Transforming Life into Literature in* Jane Eyre to mark the bicentenary of the birth of the author of that novel. The book, by Australian professor Christine Alexander and Canadian professor Sara L. Pearson, explains how Charlotte transformed the stuff of her life into a masterpiece of fiction.[4]

Other valuable additions to Brontë criticism include *A Companion to the Brontës*, which brings together essays by international scholars, both well-known and emerging, who approach the novels from different perspectives, including Marxist, feminist, postcolonial, and gender studies; and *Charlotte Brontë from the Beginnings: New Essays from the Juvenilia to the Major Works*.[5]

Modern Novels and Short Stories Inspired by the Brontë Sisters' Novels

Perhaps the most important literary work based on a Brontë work was published almost 120 years after *Jane Eyre*. Jean Rhys's 1966 novel *Wide Sargasso Sea* is what we now call a prequel. It tells the story of one of Jane's doubles, the first Mrs. Rochester, who is forced into an arranged marriage to Edward Rochester. A literary masterpiece in its own right, Rhys's novel adds "resonance to our understanding of Rochester as well as of Bertha,"[6] and also serves as a corrective to Charlotte Brontë's racially charged depiction of Bertha as less than civilized.

Two books published in 2015 similarly extend the narrative of Emily Brontë's *Wuthering Heights*. According to one review, Caryl Phillips's novel *The Lost Child* uses the original "as a symbolic conduit for ideas of alienation, orphanhood and family dislocation."[7] Although Brontë herself left Heathcliff's background "purposely mysterious," Phillips turns him into the illegitimate son of Mr. Earnshaw and an African former slave. Phillips's novel, set primarily in the twentieth century, with its focus on a University of Oxford student who drops out to marry an African Caribbean graduate student with whom she has two sons before the marriage ends, also includes a section imagining Emily on her deathbed, absorbed in "mystical death-dreams."[8]

Also published in 2015 and also riffing on *Wuthering Heights*, Alison Case's debut novel *Nelly Dean: A Return to Wuthering Heights* was favorably reviewed in *Kirkus Reviews*. Case, a professor of English literature at Williams College, provides an opportunity for housekeeper Nelly Dean to write a letter to Mr. Lockwood in which she explains points she omitted in the authentic Brontë narrative. "Her central and final revelation—about the shared parentage of important characters—is an interesting gloss on the original story." The review concludes by encouraging not only Brontë lovers but all also general fans of historical fiction to read the book, since "this well-written historical novel brings enough depth and new material to stand on its own."[9]

Nearly 170 years after the initial publication of *Jane Eyre* in 1847, a collection of twenty-one short stories inspired by "the most recognizable line in one of the world's most treasured novels," came out in 2016. Each of the contributions

dystopian

Describing a dystopia—an undesirable, frightening society.

to *Reader, I Married Him* focuses on a love story that reminds the reader of "the longings, loneliness and literary legacy" of the eponymous heroine of Charlotte Brontë's debut novel. The contributing authors themselves, hailing from different countries and backgrounds, set their stories not only in England but also in New York, Canada, Turkey, Zambia, and other locations, reflecting the fact that "Jane's story is universal to readers of every color, culture and religion." While some of the stories take place in the mid-1800s, others have cotemporary settings, and one—a dystopian tale—takes place in the distant future.[10, 11]

Nor did novelists ignore Anne Brontë. Author Sam Baker's modern version of Helen Huntingdon is a war photographer in what a reviewer described as a "fast-paced thriller" and a "disquieting, thought-provoking 21st-century take on *The Tenant of Wildfell Hall* [that] keeps twisting and turning as it hurtles towards a hair-raising climax."[12]

As enjoyable and effective as such expansions of, and riffs on, the Brontë novels may be, an article about "Current trends in Brontë criticism and scholarship" raises a compelling caveat: "While they offer opportunities for insightful recuperation, they are attended by the risk of perpetuating inaccurate impressions which might in turn delimit the range of readings of the Brontës' own works."[13] Ideally, reading such books should send readers back to the work of the sisters, not usurp them.

The Brontë Novels as Plays, Ballets, Operas

Dramatizations of Brontë are nothing new. Within a year of the publication of *Jane Eyre*, a theatrical adaptation of the novel was mounted in London. By the end of the nineteenth century, "there were at least eight strikingly different stage versions."[14] While the twentieth century did not lack for Brontë-inspired dramatizations, a number of new stage adaptations were produced during the Brontë bicentennial celebrations. Perhaps the most acclaimed was a 2015 "tumultuous re-creation" of *Jane Eyre*, a coproduction of the Bristol Old Vic and the National Theatre in London. In the words of one reviewer, the production—which begins and ends with the words "It's a girl!"—"presents a picture of exultant feminism."[15] Not only Jane but also Bertha Mason, Rochester's "mad" wife, has a voice in this passionate version, verging on madness. As of the writing of this book, the play was set to begin a tour of the United Kingdom in April 2017. Other dramatizations of *Jane Eyre* were produced in Malmo, Sweden, and in Wiesbaden, Germany, while the musical by John Caird and Paul Gordon, which premiered on Broadway in 2000, toured in Utah, Texas, and North Carolina. *The Moors*, written by playwright Jen Silverman and inspired by the lives of the three sisters, premiered off-Broadway in February 2017. Canadian audiences, meanwhile, were able to see a production of *Villette*, reviews of which were respectful but not always enthusiastic.[16]

Closer to the Brontë sisters' home, the West Yorkshire Playhouse in Leeds commissioned several new works to commemorate the bicentennial of Charlotte Brontë's birth. Having invited the commissioned artists to "approach their work from a 21st-century perspective," the theatre certainly got such an innovative approach in Yorkshire writer Linda Marshall-Griffiths's reimagining of Charlotte Brontë's *Villette*.[17] In the words of one reviewer, this dramatic version of Charlotte's final novel "catapults the action from 1853 to circa 2216," with the heroine, Lucy Snowe, depicted not as "an unassuming Victorian woman," but rather as "a clone who has survived a viral pandemic." In this version, Lucy's cloned sisters, Esme and Ash, did not survive the virus. The same review quotes the playwright, who explains her admittedly jarring interpretation of the novel:

We could have done bonnets . . . But when you're adapting or reimagining something, it's worth thinking about how this book can speak to us. Sometimes if you jump into the future it can speak back to us about who we are now . . . At the heart of *Villette*, it's about someone moving from being totally and utterly devastated back into life. It speaks so much about where we're at now because it speaks about what it means to be an outsider—and that for women and for all those people who are outsiders, the journey back in is possible.[18]

A second production by the West Yorkshire Playhouse was a rock musical about the Brontë siblings, called *Wasted*. Although set in the nineteenth century, with some characters indeed wearing bonnets, it was anything but a traditional period piece. The winner of a Kevin Spacey Foundation Arts of Choice award, the musical includes a song Charlotte sings, accompanied by guitar, in which she questions, "Why go on writing words in books when the truth is—everybody dies?"[19]

Also in celebration of the Brontë bicentennial in Yorkshire, Northern Ballet mounted dance productions of both *Jane Eyre* and *Wuthering Heights*. While a review of the former was glowing, complimenting the choreographer for developing character without sacrificing dance, a review of the latter noted the choreographer's success in "making sense of a complicated story, successfully bringing the characters to life," but regretted the supremacy of storytelling over balletic artistry.[20, 21]

Students of the lives of the Brontë sisters remember how much Charlotte and Anne enjoyed their visit to the opera in

London as guests of George Smith during their 1848 visit to clear up the questions surrounding their identity. Likewise, Brontë enthusiasts who are also opera fans had the opportunity during Charlotte's bicentennial year to enjoy the world premiere of a work, over two decades in the making, based on *Jane Eyre*. According to a news release before the October 25, 2016, opening at the Ruddock Performing Arts Centre

This 2010 ballet performance of *Wuthering Heights is* by Northern Ballet Theatre, to music composed by Claude-Michel Schönberg.

in Birmingham, John Joubert's interest in the Brontës was "sown as far back as 1969, when the composer penned his song-cycle *Six Poems of Emily Brontë*." The release also noted that Joubert's is not the first operatic treatment of Charlotte's breakthrough novel. "A previous Jane Eyre opera by Michael Berkeley and David Malouf was stolen from the composer's car in 2000. He rewrote it with lighter instrumentation."[22] The release did not, however, explain why nearly twenty years elapsed between the time the composer, John Joubert, actually completed the work in 1997, at the age of seventy, and the world premiere in 2016.

Given the popularity of the Brontë novels around the world, it is appropriate to mention that the Slovak National Theatre revived its 2014 production of *Jane Eyrová* in Bratislava in October 2016.[23]

Film and Television Adaptations of the Lives and Work of the Brontës

No discussion about the lasting legacy of the Brontës' work would be complete without mentioning film and television adaptations of the novels. Listing all of the productions would be a long and tedious process, but in the age of the Internet, one can consult a handy list covering the years 1934 through 2011 at www.imdb.com.

Several productions based not on the work but on the lives of the Brontës were scheduled to debut during the Brontë bicentennial season. Yorkshire-based Clothworkers Films' production *The Brontës*, filmed during the fall and winter of 2016, focused on "authenticity," in the words of director David Anthony Thomas: "The territory itself and the emotional resonance it has with the characters is such a key part of this story

HONORING A FILM VERSION OF A BRONTË NOVEL

In 2007 the Librarian of Congress selected William Wyler's 1939 film version of *Wuthering Heights*, starring Merle Oberon as Catherine and Laurence Olivier as Heathcliff, to be preserved in the Library of Congress's National Film Registry for its "cultural, historical, or aesthetic signficance."[24] The film misrepresents the relationship of Catherine and Heathcliff by showing them together as adults on Penistone Crag, while the novel places them on the moors only in two short passages in chapters 3 and 6, when the adolescent pair flee from Joseph's religious tirades to "have a scamper on the moors"[25] and spy on the Linton children. Despite the film's inaccuracies, its inclusion in the National Film Registry remains proof of the novel's enduring cultural impact.

that we want Haworth and the surrounding area to feature in the film as much as possible."[26]

Meanwhile, the BBC filmed, in and around Yorkshire, a new two-hour literary drama, *To Walk Invisible: The Brontë Sisters*, written and directed by Sally Wainright. According to reports in the months before the airing, "The drama revolves around the sisters' increasingly difficult relationship with Branwell, who in the last three years of his life sank into alcoholism and drug addiction,"[27] and "explores the siblings' relationship with each other and their self-educated father, who grew up in an impoverished home in rural Ireland and encouraged his children—irrespective of their gender—to become passionate about literature."[28]

In March 2016, the BBC also released a documentary on the lives of the Brontë family, *Being the Brontës*, featuring novelist Helen Oyeyemi, journalist Lucy Mangan, and news anchor Martha Kearney, who visited the Haworth Parsonage to "discover the inspiration behind [the sisters'] classic novels *Jane Eyre, Wuthering Heights,* and *Agnes Grey*."[29] Lucy Mangan, who champions Anne in the documentary, perhaps not surprisingly, identifies the presentation of the "queer little thing" (in Charlotte's dismissive words) as the most important contribution of this documentary to the twenty-first-century Brontë audience: "Why is she the underdog, the unknown Brontë, when any reading of their collected works will show her talent burning as brightly and as fiercely as those of her famous sisters? . . . I'd like to think her time has come."[30] Writing a

The Brontë sisters' appeal has not diminished over time. Each year, thousands of visitors travel to their hometown of Haworth in Yorkshire.

few days later for the *Telegraph*, Mangan pushes back again against the Brontë myth: "Anne is known as the quiet one, if she is known at all. Not passionate. Not revolutionary. Except that both her books—*Agnes Grey* and *The Tenant of Wildfell Hall*—give the lie to that."[31]

The Brontës' Lasting Imprint on Popular as well as "Elite" Culture

The late twentieth century witnessed some irreverent spinoffs of *Wuthering Heights* that demonstrate the extent to which it has been taken over by popular culture. For example, British singer Kate Bush based her 1978 pop song on the novel. Despite the banal lyrics—"Heathcliff, it's meee, Cath-eeey, come home now"—the song remained number one for a month.[32] The comedy group Monty Python's *Withering Looks*, performed in the late 1980s, exemplifies how the lives and the works of the Brontës have been intertwined. In one of its satirical songs, "It's No Life Being a Ghost," the sisters complain about all the attention heaped on them only now: "all my life I was repressed/and now I'm dead I get no rest."[33]

In the twenty-first century, fans not only of Emily but also of Charlotte and Anne can feed their enthusiasm by selecting among dozens of tchotchkes and miscellaneous kitsch available online as "Unique Emily Brontë Related Items," "Unique Charlotte Brontë Related Items," "Unique Brontë Sisters Related Items," "Unique Jane Eyre Related Items," "Unique Emily Bronte Book Related Items," and the like.

From the vantage point of the second decade of the twenty-first century, it seems fair to say that the legacy of the Brontë sisters will continue to endure, in both highbrow and lowbrow culture, and in disparate cultures, not only Anglophone ones. The characters, landscapes, and plots created by this talented family have impressed themselves so firmly on world culture that they are unlikely to be forgotten anytime soon. As long as books continue to be read, the novels of these women are likely to prove disappointing only because there are so few of them and because they all eventually must come to an end.

CHRONOLOGY

1814— April 23: Maria is born to clergyman Patrick Brontë and his wife, Maria Branwell Brontë.

1815— February 8: Elizabeth is born.

1816— Patrick Brontë's *The Cottage in the Wood* is published, the first of all the Brontë books to bear the family name spelled with the accent over the last letter; April 21: Charlotte is born.

1817— June 26: Patrick Branwell is born.

1818— July 30: Emily is born.

1820— January 17: Anne is born; April: the Brontë family moves to the parsonage in Haworth, where Patrick becomes curate.

1821— September 15: Maria Branwell Brontë dies at thirty-eight probably of cancer.

1824— Maria, Elizabeth, Charlotte, and Emily are enrolled at the Clergy Daughters' School at Cowan Bridge.

1825— May 6: Maria dies at home of tuberculosis; June 15: Elizabeth dies at home of tuberculosis; Charlotte and Emily return home.

1826— Patrick's gift of a box of wooden soldiers launches the children's juvenilia.

1831–1832— Charlotte attends Roe Head School for three terms.

1834— Branwell paints two oil portraits of the four Brontë children.

1835— Charlotte joins the faculty of Miss Wooler's school; Emily and Anne attend as students.

1838— Branwell sets up as a professional portrait painter; Emily teaches at Law Hill School; Charlotte resigns from Miss Wooler's school.

1839— Charlotte receives two marriage proposals; Anne serves as governess to the Ingham family at Blake

Hall; Charlotte is a substitute governess with the Sidgwick family.

1840– Branwell becomes a clerk for the Leeds and Manchester Railway.

1840–1845– Anne serves as governess to the Robinson family at Thorp Green Hall.

1841– Charlotte spends several months as governess for the Whites of Upperwood.

1841–1847– Branwell has more than a dozen poems published in local newspapers.

1842– Charlotte and Emily study at the Pensionnat Heger in Brussels; November 29: Aunt Branwell dies.

1843– January to December: Charlotte teaches at the Pensionnat Heger in Brussels.

1843–1845– Branwell serves as tutor to the Robinsons' son Edmund at Thorp Green.

1845– Charlotte discovers a manuscript of Emily's verse and develops a plan to jointly publish the sisters' poems using pseudonyms.

1846– May: Publication of *Poems by Currer, Ellis, and Acton Bell*; July: "the Bell brothers" submit three novels for publication: *The Professor* by Charlotte, *Wuthering Heights* by Emily, and *Agnes Grey* by Anne; August: Charlotte begins writing *Jane Eyre*.

1847– Smith, Elder publishes *Jane Eyre*; Newby publishes *Wuthering Heights* and *Agnes Grey*.

1848– Newby publishes Anne's *The Tenant of Wildfell Hall*; September 24: Branwell dies; December 19: Emily dies.

1849– May 28: Anne dies; October 26: Smith, Elder publishes Charlotte's *Shirley*.

1850– December 10: Smith, Elder publishes a new edition of *Wuthering Heights* and *Agnes Grey*, including three essays by Charlotte and her edited selection of some poems by Emily and Anne.

1851— Smith, Elder again rejects Charlotte's *The Professor*; Smith, Elder employee James Taylor proposes to Charlotte.

1852— Charlotte suffers from depression and writer's block but nonetheless submits the complete manuscript for *Villette* to Smith, Elder; December 13: Arthur Bell Nicholls proposes marriage to Charlotte.

1853— January 28: Smith, Elder publishes *Villette*.

1854— June 29: Charlotte marries Arthur Bell Nicholls.

1855— March 31: Charlotte dies of tuberculosis and complications of pregnancy; April 4: Charlotte is buried in the Haworth churchyard.

1857— Smith, Elder publish Elizabeth Gaskell's *Life of Charlotte Brontë* and Charlotte's *The Professor*.

1860— "The Last Sketch" by Charlotte Brontë is published in George Smith's *Cornhill Magazine*, with an introduction by William Makepeace Thackeray.

1861— June 7: Patrick Brontë dies at the age of eighty-four.

1893— The Brontë Society is founded.

1906— December 3: Arthur Bell Nicholls dies.

1928— The Brontë Parsonage Museum opens to the public in Haworth Parsonage.

2007— William Wyler's 1939 film version of *Wuthering Heights* is designated for preservation in the Library of Congress's National Film Registry.

2008— In a survey of English readers to identify the top love stories of all time, *Wuthering Heights* ranks first and *Jane Eyre* comes in fourth.

2016— The bicentennial of Charlotte Brontë's birth is celebrated in England and beyond.

2017— The bicentennial of Branwell Brontë's birth is celebrated in England and beyond.

CHAPTER NOTES

Chapter 1. Early Deaths, Lasting Works: Introducing the Brontë Sisters

1. "The Queen at 90: Why Does She Have Two Birthdays?," CBBC Newsround, June 10, 2016, http://www.bbc.co.uk/newsround/36489213.

2. The Brontë Society, "Charlotte's Birthday Party: Celebrating Charlotte," https://www.bronte.org.uk/whats-on/254/charlottes-birthday-party-celebrating-charlotte/263.

3. John Roberts, "From Haworth to New York. How the 200th Birthday of Charlotte Brontë Will Be Celebrated," *Yorkshire Post*, February 1, 2016, http://www.yorkshirepost.co.uk/news/education/from-haworth-to-new-york-how-the-200th-birthday-of-charlotte-bronte-will-be-celebrated-1-7709034.

4. Heather Glen, ed., *The Cambridge Companion to the Brontës* (Cambridge: Cambridge University Press, 2002), p. 225.

5. Elizabeth Gaskell, *The Life of Charlotte Brontë*, quoted in Edward Chitham, *A Life of Emily Brontë* (Oxford: Blackwell Publishers, 1987), p. 197.

6. Harold Orel, ed., *The Brontës: Interviews and Recollections* (Iowa City: University of Iowa Press, 1997), p. 183.

7. Ibid., p. 32.

8. Margaret Smith, ed., *The Letters of Charlotte Brontë; With a Selection of Letters by Family and Friends* (Oxford: Clarendon Press, 1995), 1:410.

9. Christine Alexander and Margaret Smith, eds., *The Oxford Companion to the Brontës* (Oxford: Oxford University Press, 2003), s.v. "Diary Papers," p. 163.

10. Martin Wainwright, "Emily Brontë Hits the Heights in Poll to Find Greatest Love Story," *Guardian*, August 10, 2007, https://www.theguardian.com/uk/2007/aug/10/books.booksnews.

11. Smith, *The Letters of Charlotte Brontë*, 1:18–19.

12. Margaret Smith, ed., *The Letters of Charlotte Brontë; With a Selection of Letters by Family and Friends* (Oxford: Clarendon Press, 2000), 2:118.

13. Ibid., p. 383.

14. "Bronte Writing Desk Comes Home to Haworth Parsonage," BBC News, May 24, 2011, http://www.bbc.co.uk/news/mobile/uk-england-leeds-13524136.

15. Charlotte Brontë, *Jane Eyre* (London: Penguin, 2006), chap. 38, p. 517.

16. Juliet Barker, *The Brontës* (New York: St. Martin's Press, 1994), p. 271.

17. Emily Brontë, *Wuthering Heights* (London: Penguin, 2003), chap. 9, p. 82.

18. Ibid., chap. 16, p. 169.

Chapter 2. An Incubator for Authors: The Seeds of the Brontë Sisters' Earliest Work

1. Emily Badger, "The Unbelievable Rise of Single Motherhood in America over the Last Fifty Years," *Washington Post*, December 18, 2004, https://www.washingtonpost.com/news/wonk/wp/2014/12/18/the-unbelievable-rise-of-single-motherhood-in-america-over-the-last-50-years/.

2. Gretchen Livingston, "The Rise of Single Fathers: A Ninefold Increase Since 1960," Pew Research Center, July 2, 2013, http://www.pewsocialtrends.org/2013/07/02/the-rise-of-single-fathers/.

3. Juliet Barker, *The Brontës* (New York: St. Martin's Press, 1994), p. 803.

4. Harold Orel, ed., *The Brontës: Interviews and Recollections* (Iowa City: University of Iowa Press, 1997), p. 181.

5. Christine Alexander and Margaret Smith, eds., *The Oxford Companion to the Brontës* (Oxford: Oxford University Press, 2003), s.v. "Brontë, Mrs. Maria, née Branwell," p. 63.

6. Margaret Smith, ed., *The Letters of Charlotte Brontë: With a Selection of Letters by Family and Friends* (Oxford: Clarendon Press, 1995), 1:2.

7. Ibid., p. 597.

8. Elizabeth Gaskell, *The Life of Charlotte Brontë* (New York: Harper & Brothers, 1982), p. 63.

9. Ibid.

10. Barker, *The Brontës,* p. 404.

11. Alexander and Smith, *The Oxford Companion to the Brontës,* s.v. "Aykroyd, Tabitha," p. 27.

12. Ibid., s.v. "Diary Papers," p. 163.

13. Smith, *The Letters of Charlotte Brontë,* 1:593.

14. Gaskell, *The Life of Charlotte Brontë,* p. 57.

15. Barker, *The Brontës,* p. 110.

16. Ibid., p. 119.

17. Ibid., p. 118.

18. Orel, *The Brontës,* p. 182.

19. Margaret Smith, ed., *The Letters of Charlotte Brontë: With a Selection of Letters by Family and Friends* (Oxford: Clarendon Press, 2000), 2:106.

20. Barker, *The Brontës,* p. 140.

21. Smith, *The Letters of Charlotte Brontë,* 1:240.

22. Christine Alexander, ed., *The Brontës: Tales of Glass Town, Angria, and Gondal: Selected Writings* (Oxford: Oxford World Classics, 2010), pp. 33–34.

23. Gaskell, *The Life of Charlotte Brontë*, p. 89.

24. Emily Brontë, "Rosina," in Alexander, *The Brontës: Tales of Glass Town, Angria, and Gondal: Selected Writings*, p. 412.

25. Gaskell, *The Life of Charlotte Brontë*, p. 110.

26. Charlotte Brontë, "Farewell to Angria," in Alexander, *The Brontës: Tales of Glass Town, Angria, and Gondal: Selected Writings*, p. 314.

27. Smith, *The Letters of Charlotte Brontë*, 1:589.

28. Ibid., p. 591.

29. Gaskell, *The Life of Charlotte Brontë*, pp. 102–103.

30. "The Brontës' Secret Science Fiction Stories," British Library Press Release, May 11, 2011, https://www.bl.uk/press-releases/2011/may/the-bronts-secret-science-fiction-stories.

31. Clarisse Loughrey, "Charlotte Brontë 200th Anniversary: How the Brontës Created a Completely Secret Game of Thrones-Style World," *Independent*, April 21, 2016, http://www.independent.co.uk/arts-entertainment/books/news/charlotte-bronte-200th-anniversary-how-the-brontes-created-a-completely-secret-game-of-thrones-style-a6994786.html.

32. Gaskell, *The Life of Charlotte Brontë*, p. 109.

33. Ibid., p. 110.

34. Smith, *The Letters of Charlotte Brontë*, 1:114.

35. Barker, *The Brontës*, pp. 224–225.

Chapter 3. The Gender-Bending Road to Publication: From Reluctant Teachers to Aspiring Authors

1. Charlotte Brontë, "Biographical Notice of Ellis and Acton Bell," in *The Letters of Charlotte Brontë: With a Selection of Letters by Family and Friends*, ed. Margaret Smith (Oxford: Clarendon Press, 2000), 2:742.

2. Charlotte Brontë, "Prefatory Note to 'Selections from Poems by Ellis Bell,'" in Smith, *The Letters of Charlotte Brontë*, 2:753.

3. Margaret Smith, ed., *The Letters of Charlotte Brontë: With a Selection of Letters by Family and Friends* (Oxford: Clarendon Press, 1995), 1:182.

4. Edward Chitham, *A Life of Anne Brontë* (Oxford: Blackwell Publishers, 1991), p. 53.

5. Anne Brontë, "A Voice from the Dungeon," in *The Poems of Anne Brontë: A New Text and Commentary*, ed. Edward Chitham (Totowa, NJ: Rowman & Littlefield, 1979), pp. 60–61.

6. Juliet Barker, *The Brontës* (New York: St. Martin's Press, 1994), p. 281.

7. Smith, *The Letters of Charlotte Brontë*, 1:174.

8. Barker, *The Brontës,* pp. 254–255.

9. Smith, *The Letters of Charlotte Brontë*, 1:6.

10. Ibid., pp. 166–167.

11. Ibid., p. 169.

12. Ibid., pp. 178–179.

13. Ibid., p. 191.

14. Elizabeth Gaskell, *The Life of Charlotte Brontë* (New York: Harper & Brothers, 1982), p. 204.

15. Ibid., p. 206.

16. Ibid., p. 192.
17. Smith, *The Letters of Charlotte Brontë*, 1:268.
18. Ibid., p. 269.
19. Edward Chitham, *The Birth of "Wuthering Heights": Emily Brontë at Work* (New York: St. Martin's Press, 1998), p. 56.
20. Helen MacEwan, *The Brontës in Brussels* (London: Peter Owen, 2014), pp. 52–53.
21. Smith, *The Letters of Charlotte Brontë*, 1:320.
22. Gaskell, *The Life of Charlotte Brontë*, p. 278.
23. Smith, *The Letters of Charlotte Brontë*, 1:17.
24. Ibid., p. 341.
25. Charlotte Brontë, "Biographical Notice of Ellis and Acton Bell," in Smith, *The Letters of Charlotte Brontë*, 2:743.
26. Chitham, *A Life of Anne Brontë*, p. 118.
27. Barker, *The Brontës*, p. 475.
28. Nick Holland, *In Search of Anne Brontë* (Stroud, Gloucestershire: History Press, 2016), p. 153.
29. Charlotte Brontë, "Biographical Notice of Ellis and Acton Bell," in Smith, *The Letters of Charlotte Brontë*, 2:742.
30. Holland, *In Search of Anne Brontë*, p. 156.
31. Ibid., p. 161.
32. Ibid., pp. 161–162.
33. Emily Brontë, "Faith and Despondency," in *The Poems of Emily Brontë*, ed. Derek Roper with Edward Chitham (Oxford: Clarendon Press, 1995), pp. 156–158.
34. Smith, *The Letters of Charlotte Brontë*, 1:19.

Chapter 4. The Breakthrough Book: Currer Bell's *Jane Eyre*

1. Elizabeth Gaskell, *The Life of Charlotte Brontë* (New York: Harper & Brothers, 1982), pp. 320–321.

2. Charlotte Brontë, "Biographical Notice of Ellis and Acton Bell," in *The Letters of Charlotte Brontë: With a Selection of Letters by Family and Friends*, ed. Margaret Smith (Oxford: Clarendon Press, 2000), 2:744.

3. George M. Smith, "Charlotte Brontë," *Cornhill Magazine*, New Series, vol. 9 (December 1900), pp. 78–795. Reprinted in Harold Orel, ed., *The Brontës: Interviews and Recollections* (Iowa City: University of Iowa Press, 1997), pp. 87, 90.

4. Orel, *The Brontës,* p. 107.

5. Brontë, "Biographical Notice of Ellis and Acton Bell," in Smith, *The Letters of Charlotte Brontë*, 2:744.

6. Debra Teachman, *Understanding "Jane Eyre": A Student Casebook to Issues, Sources, and Historical Documents* (Westport, CT: Greenwood Press, 2001), p. 2.

7. Charlotte Brontë, *Jane Eyre* (London: Penguin, 2006), chap. 1, p. 13.

8. Ibid., chap. 2, p. 15.

9. Ibid., chap. 3, p. 31.

10. Ibid., chap. 23, p. 292.

11. Ibid., chap. 4, p. 40.

12. Ibid., chap. 7, p. 79.

13. Ibid., chap. 8, p. 84.

14. Ibid., chap. 8, p. 88.

15. Ibid., chap. 8, pp. 82, 83.

16. Ibid., chap. 9, p. 97.

17. Ibid., chap. 10, pp. 100, 101.

18. Ibid., chap. 3, p. 30.

19. Ibid., chap. 10, p. 102.

20. Ibid., chap. 10, p. 110.

21. Ibid., chap. 27, p. 353.

22. Ibid., chap. 27, p. 365.
23. Ibid., chap. 12, pp. 129–130.
24. Ibid., chap. 11, pp. 126, 127.
25. Ibid., chap. 12, p. 130.
26. Adrienne Rich, "Jane Eyre: The Temptations of a Motherless Woman," in Jane Eyre: *An Authoritative Text, Contexts, Criticism,* ed. Richard J. Dunn (New York: Norton, 2001), p. 476.
27. Brontë, *Jane Eyre,* chap. 12, p. 129.
28. Ibid., chap. 26, p. 338.
29. Sandra M. Gilbert and Susan Gubar, *The Madwoman in the Attic: The Woman Writer and the Nineteenth-Century Literary Imagination* (New Haven, CT: Yale University Press, 1979).
30. Brontë, *Jane Eyre,* chap. 17, p. 203.
31. Ibid., chap. 29, p. 396.
32. Ibid., chap. 34, p. 467.
33. Ibid, chap. 34, p. 471.
34. Ibid., chap. 35, p. 477.
35. Ibid., chap. 35, p. 482.
36. Ibid., chap. 35, p. 483.
37. Ibid., chap. 35, p. 484.
38. Ibid., chap. 37, p. 514.
39. Ibid., chap. 37, p. 515.
40. Claire Harman, *Charlotte Brontë: A Fiery Heart* (New York: Knopf, 2015), pp. 388–389.
41. Ibid., p. 389.
42. Brontë, *Jane Eyre,* chap. 38, p. 520.
43. Gaskell, *The Life of Charlotte Brontë,* p. 347.

Chapter 5. A One-of-a-Kind Novel: Ellis Bell's *Wuthering Heights*

1. Emily Brontë, *Wuthering Heights* (London: Penguin, 2003), vol. 1, chap. 1, p. 4.

2. Charlotte Brontë, "Editor's Preface to the New Edition of Wuthering Heights," in *The Letters of Charlotte Brontë: With a Selection of Letters by Family and Friends*, ed. Margaret Smith (Oxford: Clarendon Press, 2000), 2:749.

3. Christine Alexander and Margaret Smith, eds., *The Oxford Companion to the Brontës* (Oxford: Oxford University Press, 2003), s.v. "Brontë, Emily Jane," p. 96.

4. Elizabeth Gaskell, *The Life of Charlotte Brontë* (New York: Harper & Brothers, 1982), p. 166.

5. Patsy Stoneman, ed., *Columbia Critical Guides: Emily Brontë "Wuthering Heights"* (New York: Columbia University Press, 2000), p. 12.

6. Ibid., p. 15.

7. "Appendix: Reminiscences of Charlotte Brontë by 'a Schoolfellow,'" in *The Letters of Charlotte Brontë: With a Selection of Letters by Family and Friends*, ed. Margaret Smith (Oxford: Clarendon Press, 1995), 1:600.

8. Smith, *The Letters of Charlotte Brontë*, 1:19.

9. Edward Chitham, *A Life of Emily Brontë* (Oxford: Blackwell Publishers, 1987), p. 187.

10. Edward Chitham, *The Birth of "Wuthering Heights": Emily Brontë at Work* (New York: St. Martin's Press, 1998), p. 86.

11. Q. D. Leavis, "A Fresh Approach to 'Wuthering Heights,'" in *New Casebooks: "Wuthering Heights,"* ed. Patsy Stoneman (New York: St. Martin's Press, 1993), p. 24.

12. Frank Kermode, "'Wuthering Heights' as Classic," in Stoneman, *New Casebooks: "Wuthering Heights,"* p. 39.

13. Brontë, "Editor's Preface to the New Edition of Wuthering Heights," in Smith, *The Letters of Charlotte Brontë*, 2:750.

14. Brontë, *Wuthering Heights*, vol. 1, chap. 3, p. 25.

15. Charles Percy Sanger, "The Structure of Wuthering Heights," in *"Wuthering Heights": An Authoritative Text, Backgrounds, Criticism*, 3rd. ed., ed. William M. Sale Jr. and Richard J. Dunn (New York: Norton, 1990), p. 332.

16. Brontë, *Wuthering Heights*, vol. 1, chap. 14, p. 153.

17. Ibid., vol. 1, chap. 9, p. 81.

18. Ibid., vol. 1, chap. 9, p. 83.

19. Ibid., vol. 1, chap. 9, p. 80.

20. Ibid., vol. 2, chap. 2, p. 168.

21. J. Hillis Miller, "Wuthering Heights: Repetition and the 'Uncanny,'" in Sale and Dunn, *"Wuthering Heights": An Authoritative Text, Backgrounds, Criticism*, p. 381.

22. Brontë, *Wuthering Heights*, vol. 1, chap. 1, p. 4.

23. Ibid., vol. 1, chap. 14, p. 146.

24. Ibid., vol. 1, chap. 6, p. 48.

25. Ibid., vol. 1, chap. 4, p. 37.

26. Ibid., vol. 1, chap. 4, p. 38.

27. Ibid.

28. Ibid., vol. 1, chap. 4, p. 36.

29. Ibid., vol. 1, chap. 4, pp. 36–37.

30. Ibid., vol. 1, chap. 6, p. 50.

31. Ibid., vol. 2, chap. 20, p. 330.

32. Ibid., vol. 1, chap. 13, p. 136.

33. Ibid., vol. 2, chap. 20, p. 337.

34. Chitham, *A Life of Emily Brontë*, p. 189.

35. Ibid., p. 158.

36. Brontë, "Biographical Notice of Ellis and Acton Bell," in Smith, *The Letters of Charlotte Brontë*, 2:745.

37. Chitham, *The Birth of "Wuthering Heights,"* p. 194.

Chapter 6. Last but Not Least: Acton Bell's Two Novels

1. Christine Alexander and Margaret Smith, eds., *The Oxford Companion to the Brontës* (Oxford: Oxford University Press, 2003), s.v. "'My Angria and the Angrians,'" p. 333.

2. Margaret Smith, ed., *The Letters of Charlotte Brontë: With a Selection of Letters by Family and Friends* (Oxford: Clarendon Press, 1995), 1:189.

3. Charlotte Brontë, "Biographical Notice of Ellis and Acton Bell," in *The Letters of Charlotte Brontë: With a Selection of Letters by Family and Friends*, ed. Margaret Smith (Oxford: Clarendon Press, 2000), 2:746.

4. Ellen Nussey, "Appendix," in Smith, *The Letters of Charlotte Brontë*, 1:598.

5. Drew Lamonica, *"We Are Three Sisters": Self and Family in the Writing of the Brontës* (Columbia: University of Missouri Press, 2003), p. 118.

6. Emily Brontë, *Wuthering Heights* (London: Penguin, 2003), vol. 1, chap. 5, p. 42.

7. Anne Brontë, *Agnes Grey* (Oxford: Shakespeare Head Brontë, v. 9, 1931), chap. 23, p. 205.

8. Elizabeth Gaskell, *The Life of Charlotte Brontë* (New York: Harper & Brothers, 1982), p. 192.

9. Charlotte Brontë, *Shirley* (London: Penguin Classics, 2006), chap. 12, p. 205.

10. Brontë, *Agnes Grey*, chap. 5, p. 57.

11. Ibid., chap. 7, pp. 78–79.

12. Ibid., chap. 5, p. 56.

13. Nick Holland, *In Search of Anne Brontë* (Stroud, Gloucestershire: History Press, 2016), p. 128.

14. Brontë, *Agnes Grey*, chap. 25, pp. 218–219.
15. Juliet Barker, *The Brontës* (New York: St. Martin's Press, 1994), p. 455.
16. Ibid., p. 341.
17. Ibid., p. 342.
18. Barker, *The Brontës,* p. 532.
19. Brontë, *Wuthering Heights*, vol. 1, chap. 17, p. 178.
20. Anne Brontë, *The Tenant of Wildfell Hall* (Oxford: World's Classics, 1993), chap. 14, p. 109.
21. Ibid., chap. 14, p. 110.
22. Ibid., chap. 15, p. 121.
23. Ibid., chap. 15, p. 122.
24. Patricia Ingham, *The Brontës* (Oxford: Oxford University Press, 2006), p. 153.
25. Smith, *The Letters of Charlotte Brontë*, 2:112.
26. Harold Orel, ed., *The Brontës: Interviews and Recollections* (Iowa City: University of Iowa Press, 1997), p. 91.
27. Smith, *The Letters of Charlotte Brontë*, 2:115.
28. Ibid., p. 94.

Chapter 7. Marriage and a Mission: Shaping the Family's Literary Reputation

1. Philip Rhodes, "A Medical Appraisal of the Brontës," *Brontë Society Transactions 1972*, quoted in Nick Holland, *In Search of Anne Brontë* (Stroud, Gloucestershire: History Press, 2016), p. 257.
2. Margaret Smith, ed., *The Letters of Charlotte Brontë: With a Selection of Letters by Family and Friends* (Oxford: Clarendon Press, 2000), 2:122.
3. Ibid., p. 155.
4. Ibid., p. 195.

5. Edward Chitham, *A Life of Anne Brontë* (Oxford: Blackwell Publishers, 1991), p. 178.

6. Smith, *The Letters of Charlotte Brontë*, 2:216.

7. Ibid., p. 220.

8. Ibid., p. 224.

9. Ibid., p. 232.

10. Charlotte Brontë, *Shirley* (London: Penguin Classics, 2006), chap. 16, p. 275.

11. Elizabeth Gaskell, *The Life of Charlotte Brontë* (New York: Harper & Brothers, 1982), p. 425.

12. Ibid., p. 281.

13. Brontë, *Shirley*, chap. 10, pp. 168–169.

14. Ibid., chap. 7, p. 95.

15. Smith, *The Letters of Charlotte Brontë*, 2:392.

16. Ibid., p. 241.

17. Ibid., p. 463.

18. Edward Chitham, *The Birth of* Wuthering Heights: *Emily Brontë at Work* (New York: St. Martin's Press, 1998), p. 73.

19. Chitham, *A Life of Anne Brontë*, p. 14.

20. Elizabeth Langland, *Anne Brontë: The Other One* (Houndmills, Basingstoke, Hampshire, UK: Macmillan Education Ltd., 1989), p. 29.

21. Smith, *The Letters of Charlotte Brontë*, 2:463.

22. Langland, *Anne Brontë*, p. 54.

23. Juliet Barker, *The Brontës* (New York: St. Martin's Press, 1994), p. 655.

24. William M. Sale Jr and Richard J. Dunn, eds., *Wuthering Heights* (New York: Norton, 1990), p. xi.

25. Charlotte Brontë, "Biographical Notice of Ellis and Acton Bell," in Smith, *The Letters of Charlotte Brontë*, 2:745.

26. Charlotte Brontë, "Editor's Preface to the New Edition of Wuthering Heights," in Smith, *The Letters of Charlotte Brontë*, 2:750.

27. Brontë, "Biographical Notice of Ellis and Acton Bell," in Smith, *The Letters of Charlotte Brontë*, 2:747.

28. Ibid.

29. Barker, *The Brontës*, p. 657.

30. Charlotte Brontë, *Villette* (London: Penguin Classics, 2006), chap. 27, p. 342.

31. Smith, *The Letters of Charlotte Brontë*, 2:720.

32. Margaret Smith, ed., *The Letters of Charlotte Brontë: With a Selection of Letters by Family and Friends* (Oxford: Clarendon Press, 2004), 3:28–29.

33. Ibid., p. 74.

34. Brontë, *Villette*, chap. 42, p. 543.

35. Charles McGrath, "Endings Without Endings," *New York Times*, June 17, 2007, http://www.nytimes.com/2007/06/17/weekinreview/17mcgr.html?scp=1&sq=end.

36. Smith, *The Letters of Charlotte Brontë*, 3:63.

37. Harold Orel, ed., *The Brontës: Interviews and Recollections* (Iowa City: University of Iowa Press, 1997), pp. 106–107.

38. Margaret Smith, ed., *The Letters of Charlotte Brontë: With a Selection of Letters by Family and Friends* (Oxford: Clarendon Press, 1995), 1:187.

39. Ibid., p. 198.

40. Smith, *The Letters of Charlotte Brontë*, 2:609.

41. Ibid., p. 557.

42. Smith, *The Letters of Charlotte Brontë*, 3:93.

43. Ibid., p. 250.

44. Orel, *The Brontës*, p. 129.

45. Smith, *The Letters of Charlotte Brontë*, 3:242.

46. Ibid., p. 301.

47. Miriam Phillips, "Hyperemesis Gravidarum: 'Kate Middleton's Ongoing Condition Is Much Worse Than Just Morning Sickness,'" *Guardian*, September 27, 2014, https://www.theguardian.com/uk-news/she-said/2014/sep/27/hyperemesis-gravidarum-kate-middletons-ongoing-condition-is-much-worse-than-just-morning-sickness.

48. Smith, *The Letters of Charlotte Brontë*, 3:312.

49. Ibid., p. 319.

50. Ibid., p. 326.

51. Ibid., p. 335.

Chapter 8. Charlotte Brontë's Male Survivors: Turning Over the Family's History to Others

1. Christine Nelson, *The Brontës: A Family Writes* (New York: Scala Arts, 2016), p. 86.

2. Alan H. Adamson, *Mr. Charlotte Brontë: The Life of Arthur Bell Nicholls* (Montreal & Kingston: McGill-Queen's University Press, 2008), p. 114.

3. Juliet Barker, *The Brontës* (New York: St. Martin's Press, 1994), p. 781.

4. Ibid., p. 792.

5. Charlotte Brontë, "Biographical Notice of Ellis and Acton Bell," in *The Letters of Charlotte Brontë: With a Selection of Letters by Family and Friends*, ed. Margaret Smith (Oxford: Clarendon Press, 2000), 2:747.

6. Letter from Elizabeth Gaskell to George Smith, June 4, 1855, quoted in Barker, *The Brontës*, p. 782.

7. July 1857 review, *Christian Rembrancer*, quoted in Barker, *The Brontës*, p. 796.

8. Letter from Patrick Brontë to Elizabeth Gaskell, July 30, 1857, quoted in Barker, *The Brontës,* pp. 803–804.

9. Smith, *The Letters of Charlotte Brontë,* 2:572–573.

10. Dr. Gillian Dow, "Reading, Writing, and Emma," PBS.org, http://www.pbs.org/wgbh/masterpiece/emma/reading.html (accessed November 16, 2016).

11. Charlotte Cory, "Emma Brown by Clare Boylan," *Independent,* September 12, 2003, http://www.independent.co.uk/arts-entertainment/books/reviews/emma-brown-by-clare-boylan-86630.html.

12. Harold Orel, ed., *The Brontës: Interviews and Recollections* (Iowa City: University of Iowa Press, 1997), p. 108.

13. Margaret Smith, ed., *The Letters of Charlotte Brontë: With a Selection of Letters by Family and Friends* (Oxford: Clarendon Press, 2004), 3:250.

14. Barker, *The Brontës,* p. 786.

15. Hannah Furness, "National Portrait Gallery to Reveal Mysteries of Shadowy Bronte Brother," *Telegraph,* December 18, 2015, http://www.telegraph.co.uk/culture/art/art-news/12057053/National-Portrait-Gallery-to-reveal-mysteries-of-shadowy-Bronte-brother.html.

Chapter 9. Into the Twenty-First Century and Beyond: The Brontë Sisters' Enduring Legacy

1. "Will & Jane: Shakespeare and the Cult of Celebrity," Folger Shakespeare Library, www.folger.edu/exhibitions/will-and-jane (accessed November 16, 2016).

2. "*Wild Genius on the Moors: The Story of Three Sisters* by Juliet Barker," *Kirkus,* https://www.kirkusreviews.com/book-reviews/juliet-barker/brontes/ (accessed November 16, 2016).

3. "The Brontë Sisters: The Brief Lives of Charlotte, Emily, and Anne by Catherine Reef," Kirkus, https://www.kirkusreviews.com/book-reviews/catherine-reef/bronte-sisters/ (accessed November 16, 2016).

4. Brontë Society, "Parsonage Unwrapped: Celebrating Charlotte Brontë with Christine Alexander," https://www.bronte.org.uk/whats-on/265/parsonage-unwrapped-celebrating-charlotte-bronte-with-christine-alexander/274 (accessed November 16, 2016).

5. Diane Long Hoeveler and Deborah Denenholz Morse, A Companion to the Brontës (New York: Wiley, 2016); Judith E. Pike and Lucy Morrison, eds., Charlotte Brontë from the Beginnings: New Essays from Juvenilia to the Major Works (Oxford: Routledge, 2017).

6. Patsy Stoneman, "Adaptations, Prequels, Sequels, Translations," in The Brontës in Context, ed. Marianne Thormählen, (Cambridge: Cambridge University Press, 2012), p. 209.

7. Lucasta Miller, "The Lost Child by Caryl Phillips Review—from Heathcliff to the 1960s," Guardian, April 18, 2015, https://www.theguardian.com/books/2015/apr/18/the-lost-child-caryl-phillips-review-wuthering-heights-emily-bronte.

8. Ibid.

9. "Nelly Dean: A Return to Wuthering Heights by Alison Case," Kirkus, https://www.kirkusreviews.com/book-reviews/alison-case/nelly-dean/ (accessed November 16, 2016).

10. Carol Memmott, "Reader, I Married Him Collects 21 Writings on Brontë's Jane Eyre," Chicago Tribune, March 24, 2016, http://www.chicagotribune.com/lifestyles/

books/ct-prj-reader-i-married-him-jane-eyre-tracy-chevalier-20160324-story.html.

11. Tracy Chevalier, ed., *"Reader, I Married Him": Stories Inspired by* Jane Eyre (New York: HarperCollins, 2016).

12. Samantha Ellis, "*The Woman Who Ran* by Sam Baker Review—21st-Century Take on *The Tenant of Wildfell Hall*," *Guardian*, January 29, 2016, https://www.theguardian.com/books/2016/jan/29/the-woman-who-ran-by-sam-baker-review-the-tenant-of-wildfell-hall.

13. Alexandra Lewis, "Current Trends in Brontë Criticism and Scholarship," p. 204.

14. Stoneman, "Adaptations, Prequels, Sequels, Translations," in Thormählen, *The Brontës* in Context, p. 207.

15. Susannah Clapp, "Jane Eyre Review—Aflame with Passion and Madness," *Guardian*, September 27, 2015, https://www.theguardian.com/stage/2015/sep/27/jane-eyre-lyttleton-national-theatre-review-sally-cookson-passion-and-madness.

16. Maighdlin Mahoney, "Review: *Villette* (Amicus Production)," February 13, 2016, http://www.mooneyontheatre.com/2016/02/13/review-villette-amicus-productions/.

17. David Knights, "Brontë Season Announced at West Yorkshire Playhouse in Leeds," *Keighley News*, April 27, 2016, http://www.keighleynews.co.uk/news/charlottebronte/14455021.Bront___season_announced_at_West_Yorkshire_Playhouse_in_Leeds/.

18. Ian Youngs, "Reinventing the Brontë Sisters for the 22nd Century," BBC.com, September 28, 2016, http://www.bbc.com/news/entertainment-arts-37473528.

19. Ibid.

20. Rachel Ward, "Northern Ballet's New Jane Eyre Is a Beautiful and Expressive Tribute to Brontë—Review," *Telegraph*, June 1, 2016, http://www.telegraph.co.uk/dance/what-to-see/jane-eyre-northern-balletrichmond-theatre-review-a-beautiful-and/.

21. "Northern Ballet: Wuthering Heights—West Yorkshire Playhouse, Leeds," Reviews Hub, July 9, 2016, http://www.thereviewshub.com/northern-ballet-wuthering-heights-west-yorkshire-playhouse-leeds/.

22. Norman Lebrecht, "It's Jane Eyre the Opera—Again," Slippedisc.com, July 11, 2016, http://slippedisc.com/2016/07/its-jane-eyre-the-opera-again/.

23. "Charlotte Bronte: Jane Eyre," Slovak National Theatre, http://www.snd.sk/?drama&predstavenie=03_jana&termin=6460 (accessed November 16, 2016.

24. "Librarian of Congress Announces National Film Registry Selections for 2007," Library of Congress, December 27, 2007, https://www.loc.gov/today/pr/2007/07-254.html.

25. Emily Brontë, *Wuthering Heights* (London: Penguin, 2003), vol. 1, chap. 3, p. 22.

26. Miran Rahman, "Producers of New Film About the Brontës Aiming to Be Faithful to History," *Keighley News*, March 3, 2016, http://www.keighleynews.co.uk/news/14317722.Producers_of_new_film_about_the_Brontes_aiming_to_be_faithful_to_history/.

27. Joanna Crawley, "Sister Act: Filming Begins on BBC's Lavish New Bronte Drama *To Walk Invisible* as Cast Take Over York in Their Beautiful Period Costumes," *Daily Mail*, May 19, 2016, http://www.dailymail.co.uk/tvshowbiz/article-3599403/Sister-act-Filming-begins-BBC-s-lavish-new-Bronte-drama-Walk-Invisible-cast-York-beautiful-period-costumes.html.

28. PA and *Telegraph* reporters, "BBC to Dramatise the Lives of the Bronte Sisters," BBC.com, May 18, 2015, http://www. telegraph.co.uk/culture/tvandradio/11612791/BBC-to-dramatise-the-lives-of-the-Bronte-sisters.html.

29. "Being the Brontes," BBC, http://www.bbc.co.uk/programmes/p03kcd3l (accessed November 16, 2016).

30. Lucy Mangan, "The Forgotten Genius: Why Anne Wins the Battle of the Brontes," *Guardian*, March 23, 2016, https://www.theguardian.com/books/2016/mar/23/being-the-brontes-bbc-lucy-mangan-anne-bronte.

31. Lucy Mangan, "What the Brontë Sisters Were Really Like," *Telegraph,* March 26, 2016, http://www.telegraph.co.uk/tv/2016/03/25/what-the-bronte-sisters-were-really-like.

32. "Sold on Song Top 100: 'Wuthering Heights,' Kate Bush," BBC, n.d., http://www.bbc.co.uk/radio2/soldonsong/songlibrary/wutheringheights.shtml (accessed November 16, 2016).

33. Paula M. Krebs, "*Wuthering Heights* in the Culture of the English Department," in *Approaches to Teaching Emily Brontë's "Wuthering Heights,"* ed. Sue Lonoff and Terri A. Hasseler (New York: Modern Language Association of America, 2006), p. 85.

Literary Terms

allegory A literary form wherein characters, objects, incidents, and descriptions have both literal and figurative meanings.

anagram A word or name made by rearranging the letters of another word or name.

bildungsroman A "novel of education," which describes the personal development of a single individual from youth on.

domestic novel A novel that examines the home and family.

doubling The depiction of pairs of characters to highlight similarities or differences between them.

dystopian An adjective that describes a dystopia—an undesirable, frightening society.

epic poem A very long poem that recounts the adventures of a central heroic figure.

epistolary novel A novel whose story is told through letters.

eponymous Referring to being the person or thing after whom something is named.

fan fiction A piece of writing based on characters from an original work of fiction, written by fans of the original work.

Gothic novel A novel characterized by horror, violence, and supernatural effects, usually set against a background of a gloomy and isolated castle.

juvenilia Writings produced during childhood.

novel of manners A novel that realistically depicts the customs, behaviors, habits, and expectations of a social group.

Victorian A term used to refer to traits associated with English society during the long reign of Queen Victoria (1837–1901), including prudishness and conventionality.

Major Works by
THE BRONTË SISTERS

Currer, Ellis, and Acton Bell (Charlotte, Emily, and Anne Brontë)

Poems (1846)

Anne Brontë

Agnes Grey (1847)
The Tenant of Wildfell Hall (1848)

Charlotte Brontë

Jane Eyre (1847)
Shirley (1849)
Villette (1853)
The Professor (1857)

Emily Brontë

Wuthering Heights (1847)

FURTHER READING

Alexander, Christine, and Margaret Smith. *The Oxford Companion to the Brontës*. Oxford: Oxford University Press, 2006.

Barker, Juliet. *The Brontës: Wild Genius on the Moors: The Story of a Literary Family*. New York: Pegasus, 2012.

Barnard, Robert, and Louise Barnard. *A Brontë Encyclopedia*. Hoboken, NJ: Wiley-Blackwell, 2007.

Harman, Claire. *Charlotte Brontë: A Fiery Heart*. New York: Knopf, 2015.

Holland, Nick. *In Search of Anne Brontë*. Gloucestershire, UK: History Press, 2016.

Reef, Catherine. *The Brontë Sisters: The Brief Lives of Charlotte, Emily, and Anne*. New York: Clarion Books, 2012.

WEBSITES

The Brontë Blog
bronteblog.blogspot.com
Contains links to e-texts by the Brontës, e-texts on the Brontës, Brontë Stuff Online, Reviews, Brontës in the News, and Recent and Upcoming Books.

The Brontë Parsonage Museum & Brontë Society
www.bronte.org.uk
Contains information about the organization and museum, descriptions of the museum and library collection, biographical information about the Brontës and the circle in Haworth, and updates on museum events and the contemporary arts program at the museum.

Poetry Foundation
www.poetryfoundation.org/poems-and-poets/poets
Contains links to the sisters' poems and comments by other authors about them.

Victorian Web
www.victorianweb.org/authors/bronte
Contains links to work by and about each of the sisters.

INDEX

Nicholls, Arthur Bell, 11, 128–130, 132, 137–138, 139, 140, 141, 142–143
Nussey, Ellen, 23, 24, 26, 36, 38, 39, 42, 44, 48, 52, 82, 98, 106, 115, 117, 126, 127, 128, 129–130, 132, 134, 142–143
Nussey, Henry, 127

O

Oroonoko, 12

P

Paradise Lost, 21, 77
Pensionnat Heger, 50
Pilgrim's Progress, 21
Ponden Hall, 82–83
Poole, Grace, 68, 70
"Prefatory Note to 'Selections from Poems by Ellis Bell,'" 121
Professor, The, 58, 60–61, 100, 123, 137–138
Pryce, Reverend David, 127

R

Reed family, 63, 65
Revelation, book of, 74, 77
Rhys, Jean, 148–149
Rich, Adrienne, 70
Rivers, St. John, 72–74, 77
Robinson Crusoe, 12
Robinson family, 45, 52–53, 105–106
Rochester, Edward Fairfax, 34, 68–70, 72, 73–74, 75, 76, 77, 101
Roe Head School, 35–36, 38, 41, 42, 44, 45

S

Scarborough, 117
Scatcherd, Miss, 65–66
Shirley, 99, 101, 118–119
Shorter, Clement King, 142–143
Smith, Elder and Company, 54, 60–61, 62, 121, 123, 124, 134, 137–138

Smith, George, 60, 61, 111, 112, 123, 124, 128, 138, 140
Snowe, Lucy, 123, 124–125
Southey, Robert, 46, 47
spiritual pilgrimage, 21, 63, 77

T

Taylor, James, 127
Taylor, Mary, 28, 36, 110, 112, 119
Temple, Miss, 65–66, 67
Tenant of Wildfell Hall, The, 14, 98, 99, 105–110, 121
Thackeray, William Makepeace, 61, 126–127, 139–140
Thornfield, 68–70, 74, 101
Thorp Green, 105–106
Thrushcross Grange, 86, 89–90
"triple-decker," 62, 83, 102, 105

V

Varens, Adèle, 68, 101
Victoria, Queen of England, 16–17
Villette, 123–124, 126–127

W

Waterloo, Battle of, 31
Wellington, Duke of, 30–32
White, Mr. and Mrs. John, 48–49
Wide Sargasso Sea, 148–149
Wiggins, Patrick Benjamin, 96
Williams, W. S., 13, 60–61, 62, 112, 114, 115, 117, 118, 119, 121, 124, 138
Winkworth, Catherine, 129
Wooler, Margaret, 35, 36, 38, 44, 45, 124, 129
Wuthering Heights, 14, 15–16, 17, 60, 79, 81–83, 84, 85–86, 87, 89–90, 91, 95, 99, 107, 108–109, 121–122, 149, 155

Y

Yorkshire, 7–8, 23, 26, 87–88, 92, 155, 156